# Consume Me

Master Chefs #3

Kailin Gow

**Consume Me (The Master Chefs Series #3)**

Consume Me (The Master Chefs Series #3)
Published by Sparklesoup Inc.


For information, please contact:

Sparklesoup Inc.
www.sparklesoup.com

# DEDICATION

To my readers, thank you! If you love this story, this wouldn’t be possible without your love and support!

# Prologue

The lunch rush at Sam's Restaurant went off without a hitch and Taryn Cummings quickly shifted gear and prepared for the dinner crowd. She'd barely had time to sit down, had only taken a quick chomp of a carrot stick, and hadn't even gone to the bathroom yet. She took a minute to breathe, collect herself and get going again.

Thank goodness she had Errol's staff on hand.

They were a dream to work with and she silently thanked Errol for the thousandth time for allowing them to leave their stations at his New York restaurant to come help her out.

Though Errol's restaurant had been seriously damaged by fire and his staff had been dispersed to his other restaurants, he had generously transferred a handful of them to her aid.

"I know you need a helping hand, Taryn," he'd said as he'd prepared for his flight back to France. "Your mom probably won't be up and about for a while still, and your brother has his cooking classes."

"You have no idea how I appreciate it, Errol. I think I'd be lost without them."

And as she now watched the team clear the kitchen of the midday feast and dive into the preparations for the dinner menu, she realized just how true those words were. As Darla chopped celery, Sharon prepared a wine sauce and Nigel seasoned steaks, Taryn wiped down the stainless steal counter.

"A little distracted, Tar?" Darla asked. "I think that's the fourth time you wipe the counter."

She chuckled and tossed her damp cloth into the sink of sudsy hot water. "Yeah, I guess."

"Long distance relationships are never easy."

Taryn looked quizzically at the older woman with the graying temples. She was a whiz in the kitchen; never tired, never complained, never missed a beat. And apparently knew more about her personal life than she let on.

She'd never mentioned anything about her relationship with Errol and even less about her feelings since he'd left for Europe.

"It's not very hard to see, sweetheart," Darla went on as she efficiently chopped the celery into consistently sized pieces. "You have that unmistakable lovelorn, lost puppy dog look in your eyes."

"Then I guess there's no point denying it."

"How long has he been gone now, a week or so?"

"Two weeks, three days and…" Tar glanced at her watch. "Ten hours."

Darla chuckled as she reached for another stalk of celery. "Be thankful this place is so busy. Gives you a chance to think of something other than your distant love."

"I do. Everyday. I've actually surprised myself more than once… looking at the clock, happy to realize it's been over an hour since I last thought of him. Otherwise time crawls on at an excruciating pace. I mean, I know that filming that television show of his is important and everything, but…"

Darla kept her eyes on her quickly chopping knife and called out, "But…?"

Taryn shrugged and let out a childish sigh. "This is New York City, for heaven's sake. Why couldn't he just tape his show here? Why does it have to be all the way over in Paris?"

Shooting her a quick knowing glance, Darla smiled.

"Yeah, yeah," Taryn went on as she lifted her hand straight out in front of her and lovingly gazed at the diamond ring on her finger. "I know. Everything started over there… the studio kitchen is already set up… yadda, yadda, yadda. I know. I'm just being silly."

"You're just in love."

She was engaged to a handsome, rich, successful man and this was a part of his life. This was a part of him and she would just have to get accustomed to it.

Throughout the preparations for the dinner rush, she thought of him, but then the night took on a life of its own.

In addition to the reservations made well in advance, an impromptu crowd filled the restaurant to capacity. The evening flew by in a flurry of braised lamb, grilled salmon, flambéed strawberries and more wine than Taryn would have ever thought possible.

By the time closing hour arrived, she was exhausted, but thoroughly satisfied with the evening. Even with her mom still recovering from her fall and her brother Bobby off to his cooking class, she'd successfully run the restaurant the whole day. It was as close to perfect as she could hope for.

As the last of her employees as well as Errol's staff left Sam's Restaurant, Taryn leaned back against the counter and smiled. Running a restaurant was one hell of a job, but she'd never felt more invigorated and happy.

"Long day?"

Startled, she turned to the unexpected sound of the male voice. "Matt! What are you doing here?" She reached out to give him a hug.

He shrugged. "I was in the neighborhood…"

"Great. I'm really happy to see you. Want a bite to eat?"

He shook his head.

"You sure? I have a big bowl of salad. I was about to have some, and aside from that and the portion I want to take to my mom, the rest is going to go to waste." With her head she gestured toward the big stainless steel bowl on the counter. "My take on a Waldorf. It's full of almonds and dried cranberries, and of course my own secret vinaigrette."

Walking over to the bowl, he picked up a piece of lettuce and put it in his mouth. "Pretty good," he said with an impressed cock of his brow. "Maybe I will have a bit."

"Great." She patted his arm. "We can have a little chat while we eat."

She tossed the salad, bringing the almonds and cranberries that'd sunk to the bottom back up to the top, then shoveled two healthy servings into large bowls.

"I haven't seen you in a while," she said as she brought the bowls to a little table just outside the kitchen.

"Sam's is a little more out of the way since I've transferred to that new firehouse. I keep telling myself I should pop in more often, but I rarely get the chance. It's a busier neighborhood. We don't have much time to fool around." He sat down and plunged his fork into the salad.

He fidgeted, suddenly uncomfortable and silent as he ate. Taryn had known him for so long and had never seen him so agitated and ill at ease. She'd also never seen him looking so handsome and sexy. While she was very well aware of the cliché that clung to firemen, Matt was sexy in a very subdued and charming way. He almost seemed oblivious of his good looks.

Taryn caught his gaze that skimmed over her diamond ring and suddenly realized why he seemed so anxious.

"Besides, you seem to be in good hands," Matt finally added.

Though he smiled, the regret was plain in his voice. For the first time since her engagement to Errol, Taryn felt uncomfortable at the sight of her engagement ring and discretely set her hand on her lap.

"Well, I'm glad you finally took the time to come out. I've missed you." She'd felt his absence all the more since Errol had left.

He frowned as he nodded. "Actually, this isn't just a social call."

"Oh?"

He hesitated an excruciatingly long time and Taryn was about to question him when he finally met her gaze.

"I've been privy to some fire reports lately."

"Is this regarding your new position? What are you now, captain?"

He nodded. "I guess you could say that." Setting his fork down, he swallowed as a pained look came over him.

"Is something wrong?"

"Earlier today a report came to my attention; the fire report of Errol King's restaurant."

At the sound of Errol's name, Taryn's heart skipped a beat.

"It was initially believed that a faulty stove was at cause, but…"

Cocking her head to the side, she narrowed her eyes as she waited for him to go on.

"Turns out that stove was practically brand new and in perfect working condition. Nothing faulty about it. We also inspected all the wiring at the restaurant and everything was in order. The place had been fully re-wired a little while back and was up to code. His electrical system could have easily handled a few more stoves, some refrigerators and a slew of small kitchen appliances."

"Matt, what are you saying?"

"The report seemed to be leaning toward the suspicion that the fire was deliberately set."

She chuckled. "That's absurd. Errol is a celebrity and he's loved by everyone. He has no enemies, even in the culinary world. They all look up to him and revere him. No one would torch his place."

Matt sat back and looked down at his lap. "I don't think it was an enemy either."

Taryn frowned as she anticipated his next words.

"It looks like Errol may have set the fire himself."

Letting out a loud harrumph, Taryn sat up and leaned her elbows on the table. "Now, that's not just absurd, it's downright crazy. Do you have any idea who you're talking about, Matt? Do you have any idea how much blood, sweat and tears Errol has literally put into that restaurant? There is no way… no way he would ever set a match to it."

"Tar, the report says…"

"The report is wrong, Matt. You're wrong. I know him. I know he wouldn't do anything to destroy something he worked so damned hard to build."

"Tar, please listen. Despite all his hard work, and I have no doubt he did work to make this restaurant a success, things weren't really going as he'd planned. Reservations this year fell way short of what they'd forecast; way short. On top of that, Errol also opened another restaurant – *Chez Les Copains* – in Santa Monica last year. It seems to have bombed and it's draining funds from the other restaurants."

"Errol knows how to run a restaurant… a successful restaurant. If *Les Copains* was failing in California, he'd shut it down before his other restaurants were affected in any way. You must be mistaken… or whoever it is who wrote that report."

"I'm not mistaken, Tar. He can't close *Les Copains* because of his business partner who's hungry for the prestige of that location. Apparently it's the place to be seen and heard and there's no way they're going to allow it to close… even if it means trouble for the other restaurants."

Taryn shook her head in disbelief. "I still think there must be some other explanation. Errol isn't the type of man to play that sort of game. If he were having financial trouble, he'd find another way of rectifying the situation. For crying out loud, he's a world renowned chef with his own show and cookbooks."

"Do you know what he was doing the day of the fire? Were you with him?"

She huffed with exasperation. "No, I wasn't with him. We'd had a falling out and… well, I just didn't see him for a little while." She could have sworn she saw a hint of a grin come to Matt's lips.

"So he doesn't even have an alibi." He shook his head. "I really hate to be the one to have to tell you this, Tar, but this is serious. If Errol King torched his place in order to collect from the insurance company, he's in for a hell of a lot of trouble."

"You're jumping to conclusions. Just because I wasn't with him doesn't mean no one saw him."

"And I think you're in denial."

"Look, the next time I talk to him, I'll ask him where he was that night."

"You should do that." Matt put his hand on her shoulder and gave her a tender squeeze. "I really hate to see you get mixed up with the wrong type of guy."

"I'll call him first chance I get, and I'll prove to you that he's not the wrong type of guy."

Matt stood. "For your sake, I hope you're right, but from where I'm standing, things don't look too good for Mr. Errol King." He leaned in to give her a peck on the cheek. "Thanks for the salad. It was really great. I understand why this place has taken off like it has. You have a real talent for delicious food."

"Thanks, Matt."

"I'll see you around."

# Chapter 1

As Taryn drove home, she repeatedly played back Matt's words in her head. It was outrageous that he could even suggest such a thing. How could anyone look at Errol and think him an arsonist?

She meticulously went over every minute of the day of the fire. In her mind's eye, she could see the pain in Errol's face as his restaurant lay in embers behind him. He was distraught, beside himself with grief. He may as well have lost a loved one.

Once again she concluded; Matt was mistaken.

She reached her apartment and carelessly parked the car, leaving it a little askew with the back bumper slightly out in the street. Too eager to speak to Errol, she didn't want to waste another minute trying to properly squeeze the car into place. She pulled out her phone scrolled down to his name and placed the call.

"Hi, baby," he said from halfway around the world. "Your timing couldn't be better. We just wrapped up another episode and my nerves are frazzled like you wouldn't believe. Your voice is the perfect balm to such a frantic day."

"I'm glad to hear that. So what's going on with you?" She heard the eternal longing in her voice despite her attempt to hide it. She wanted him in the most desperate way and hearing his deep throaty voice made the distance between them all the more unbearable. She was already wet with desire.

"Just missing you while I work my butt off. Whoever says stardom is easy has no idea what they're talking about. Twelve, sometimes even fourteen hour days, baby."

"Poor, sweetie. What can I do to help?"

"You can just talk to me. Just the sound of your voice calms me down… well, that is most of me. A few parts only get more excited the more you talk. So bring me down from the frenzy of cooking in front of a camera and take me on a wicked journey like only you can."

"In that case, my Master Chef," she purred seductively, "I think you'd better sit down. Find a place that's nice and comfortable, a place where you can be alone, and relax, undisturbed. We may be thousands of miles apart, but baby, I want you to feel like I'm right there with you."

"I like it already." His voice was husky with anticipation.

Taryn leaned the car seat back a bit.

"I've had a murderous day at the restaurant," she said. "If you don't mind, I'd like to just get a little more comfortable."

"And what would that entail?"

"My bra is too tight and it's cinching my skin. I'm going to go under my shirt and find the bra clasp between my breasts. And voila… with a quick flick of my fingers and my breasts can breathe again."

"Are they firm?"

She reached for her breast. "Firm and aching. My nipples are hard before I even reach for them."

"Lick your fingers."

Tar pulled her hand out from under her shirt, licked her thumb and index finger and returned to pinch her nipple with the moist fingertips. "Yes, that's so much better," she growled.

"Are you wet?"

"Too wet. Let's concentrate on you for a minute. It seems like such a long time ago when I last reached into your pants and ran my finger along the length of your cock. It seems like an eternity since I pulled your hard-on out of your pants and put it deep into my mouth, sucking on it until you groaned."

He groaned in response. "Like that?"

She could hear the gentle but distinctive sound of flesh stroking fervently over flesh.

"Do you remember, Errol, the heat of my mouth, the feel of my tongue over the length of you? Do you remember what it feels like when I suck hard, then coddle you gently?"

"Yes. Damn, but you're making it all the more difficult to stay here without you," he growled. "Now, I want to feel your flesh. How hot and wet are you?"

She reached under her jeans, under her panties and slid her fingers between the inflamed folds of skin that immediately throbbed under her touch. "I'm excruciatingly hot, Errol."

"Where are you?"

"In my car, just outside my apartment."

"Hmmm, a little exhibitionism. Even hotter."

Swallowing a lump of anticipation, she considered his comment. She'd not really planned on making a spectacle of herself.

"Is your shirt open?"

She licked her lips and hesitated. "No."

"You wearing a t-shirt?"

"Yes."

"Take it off."

Silence.

"Did you take it off?"

"Hold on," she purred as she put the phone down a brief second and tugged her shirt over her head. "It's off."

"Can you see your breasts in the moonlight?"

"Yes. They're shimmering. White orbs that glow in the otherwise dark night."

"Your tits are so luxuriously big. I can just imagine them now."

"I'd love to shove them in your face, have you nuzzle between them."

"Grab them, Tar. Squeeze them tight. Lift them up so that you're almost choking on them. Can you feel how luxurious they are?"

Reveling in the sensation of her firm flesh in her hand, she groaned her pleasure. "I want you to slide your dick between my tits. I want you to cum and slather my tits." Being so far away from Errol, Taryn talked as naughty and sexy as she could, wanting the words to convey her lust for Errol. In phone sex with Errol, it was either go strong and hard or don't bother at all.

"Is anyone passing by?"

"In the distance, there's a guy coming. Hold on, there's a girl with him, too."

He hissed a deep breath. "Can he see you?"

"No. Not yet."

"Are they getting closer?"

"Yes. Now. I think he just spotted me."

"Does he see your tits?"

"Um… Yes."

Errol sucked in a deep and jagged breath. "Lucky bastard."

"He's staring at me." Her own breath was difficult to control. "His girl doesn't seem too happy, though."

"Put your hand down your pants."

Fully aroused by the sound of Errol's voice in her ear and the stranger's eyes on her, she hurried to unzip her jeans, pull them open and pull them down just enough to give the passers-by a peek. Shoving her finger deep inside the heated moisture and rubbing herself where she was heated the most, she gasped, surprised by the intensity of the long-distance orgasm that Errol was giving her.

"He just slowed down," she said through raspy breaths.

"Are you about to cum, Tar?"

"Yes."

"And I'm about to explode. Are his eyes on you?"

"Yes. He's looking straight at me. His lips are parted… He just licked his lips."

"Look directly in his eyes."

"I am."

"Do you see his hunger? His desire to have you?"

She growled. "Yes."

"Do you see my hunger for you in his eyes?"

"Yes." Staring into the man's eyes, she could see his burning desire in them, and he stopped to move a hand down to his cock, where there was an unmistakable large bulge in his pants.

"Can you feel me, Tar?"

"Yes," she shouted as her orgasm took control, and she began to shake.

He growled in her ear deeply and she knew he'd also reached that climactic moment.

Tar closed her eyes, her last vision that of the hot and bothered young man being tugged along by his angry and flustered girlfriend.

"As great as that was," Errol whispered, "it can't beat having you here in person. I want you here, Tar. I need you… bad. I want to feel you wrapped around me while I go deep into you. Why don't you take the weekend off? Go straight to the airport, get on a plane and come be with me."

Taryn considered his invitation. She couldn't deny how she longed to see him, to feel him, to hold him. The sound of his voice, and making love to him over the phone only emphasized how she missed him. Added to that were Matt's words. If she were to speak to Errol about the whole fire situation, she thought it best to do it in person.

"You know, I think I'd like that. I could just run in, see my mom a bit, pick up a few things and head straight to LaGuardia."

“I’ll call right away to make sure there’s a ticket waiting for you,” he said.

“That’d be great.”

“But, Tar…” There was a strange hint of shame and embarrassment in his voice.

“Yeah?”

“Look, since the whole thing with the fire…” He cleared his throat. “The insurance money didn’t come in like I’d expected and the remodeling is almost more expensive than building the place to begin with and it’s busting the bank. And… well… First class is a little pricey, so do you mind if…”

“Errol, of course I don’t mind. I don’t care whether I fly first class, coach or economy. Hell, I’d fly in the baggage compartment if it meant I could be with you for a few days.”

“Baby, you're amazing. That’s one of the things I love about you. You find pleasure in the simple things.”

“Well, I find a lot of pleasure in you, but you're far from simple,” she teased.

He chuckled. “Just get your ass over her as soon as you can.”

"Will do." She hung up, euphoric at the thought of seeing him. Then the wave of dread hit her.

What if Matt was right?

# Chapter 2

"Is that you, Tar?" Samantha called from her bedroom.

"Yes, Mom." Tar kicked off her shoes as her mother came out to meet her. "I brought you a little something for dinner. A bit of salad and a few grilled shrimps."

"I'm not really hungry."

"Mom, you know what the doctor said. You have to start eating a bit more." She walked to the kitchen and pulled containers of food out of a paper bag.

"I know. I will. How was everything at the restaurant?" Picking up a container of plain noodles, she took a whiff.

"Great. Everything went smoothly."

"And…?"

"And what?"

"You have that expression on your face; the one that appears whenever you have to tell me something, but don't want to tell me anything."

Taryn chuckled. "Will I ever be able to hide anything from you?"

"Maybe when I'm old and senile. So, what's on your mind?"

She turned to her mother, a confident fist propped up on her hip. "Okay, let's make a deal then. You eat a bit more than just a few mouthfuls and I'll tell you what's on my mind."

"You drive a hard bargain, daughter of mine." Sam grabbed the wide and flat platter of salad at sat at the little dinette table. "Well, you lose, honey, because I was ready to dive into this salad anyway."

Taryn pulled up a chair and sat facing her mom. "Errol is in Paris."

"Taping his cooking show. Yeah, I know honey, you told me."

"For the past weeks we've called each other a few times. It's great hearing the sound of his voice and…"

"Go to Paris, honey."

"Huh?"

"That's what you really want to do, right?"

"Yeah, but…"

"But what, honey? I'm out of commission? Bobby is in school?"

"Well, yes." She reached out to pick a piece of lettuce.

"Look, Errol or not, you need a vacation. You're not going to do anyone any favors if you collapse from exhaustion. You've been running the show on your own long enough. I'm finally back on my feet and I'd fully intended to go back to the restaurant Monday morning anyway. The timing couldn't be more perfect."

"Mom, Bobby is in school full time now. He'll hardly be there to help you… maybe a few hours on the weekend if you're lucky, but that's all."

"You still have Errol's crew helping us out, don't you?"

"Yeah."

"And they're doing a terrific job, aren't they?"

"They sure are."

"So where's the problem?" Sam speared her fork through the salad and took a big mouthful of vegetables.

Taryn smiled.

"Hmm, really good."

"Thanks."

"Your vinaigrette?"

"Yeah."

"Nice."

"Thanks."

After a few more mouthfuls, Sam looked her daughter in the eye. "You know what, honey… Errol is the kind of man who won't just sit around waiting for the next phone call. I mean phone sex can only take you so far. He'll get bored, he'll get restless, he'll get needy and he'll get laid somewhere else."

Taryn's jaw dropped open as she gaped at her mother. "Mom!" she whined.

"Don't look at me like that, sweetie. I've been around the block a time or two. I do know what men want, you know."

"I know, but…"

"Look, all I'm saying is… don't neglect him. Don't take him for granted. Don't forget that he's a strong, rich and powerful man, who needs a woman like you at his side."

Taryn nodded.

"But also make sure you don't forget the sensitive soul that he is."

"There's so much to do here," Taryn whispered. "I can't imagine leaving you to…"

Sam reached out to take her hand. "You managed to do what I'm sure hundreds of women have attempted; you broke through Errol's hard exterior and melted his loving interior. But I have a feeling that if he's away from you too long…"

"The hard exterior will come back," Tar finished.

"If he has abandonment issues, he could come to feel abandoned by you if you ignore him too long. I assume he's the one who asked you to go see him."

"He asked me to get on the next flight out."

Sam threw her fork into the salad and shot out of her chair. "Then what the hell are you doing here talking to your ole ma over a salad? Get packing and get out of here."

Taryn stared at her mother, amazed with her strength and wisdom. "Are you sure, Mom?"

Not wasting another second, Sam grabbed Taryn's arm, pulled her out of her chair and led her to her bedroom. "I'll help you pack."

Giggling, Tar sat on the edge of her bed and watched her mother. With more efficiency than she would have thought her mother capable of with her injuries, Sam pulled a small suitcase off the top shelf of Taryn's closet.

Suddenly solemn, she whispered, "Mom?"

"Yeah, sweetie." She threw the suitcase open on Taryn's bed.

"What happened to Dad?"

She froze for a moment and simply stared into the empty suitcase. "Your father had a lot of demons," she finally said. "He didn't really have the makings to be a father to anyone. Not that I'm defending him, but he didn't have an easy childhood and he was constantly haunted by his past."

She turned to open the drawers of Taryn's dresser and pulled out various articles of clothing. "I did my best to hold up my end of the bargain. I tried to raise you guys, keep you guys happy, all the while keeping you quiet… keep you out of his hair. I had to make sure he got enough rest so he wouldn't complain too much. I worked two jobs to make sure there was food on the table. Meanwhile, he drank and gambled his paychecks away."

"I remember seeing you go off to work a lot."

Sam nodded. "Your father did try. I'll give him that. For a while he had a really good paying job, not that it changed anything for me. I still had to work my butt off. Anyway, after working for this drilling company for a few months, he got a lucrative contract. He'd been invited to train a whole crew down in San Antonio. I was ecstatic. It felt like everything was finally coming together. We moved you guys down there and I thought we were finally on our way to something special."

"I think I vaguely remember that. We'd gone to visit one of the missions there, didn't we?"

Sam chuckled. *"All of them... San José, Espada, San Juan de Capistrano,* and your favorite*, La Concepcion*," she said with Latino flair. "You loved it all. The architecture, the history, the beauty."

"What happened? Why didn't we stay there?"

"We were only supposed to be there for eight months. That's how long they gave your dad to train the crew there. The money rolled in. His paychecks were huge. I could hardly believe it. We were housed and they even gave him a gas and grocery allowance, so we had little expenses. I started dreaming of everything we could do with those big paychecks."

She turned to look at Taryn. "I wanted a house. I had never even dreamed of the possibility before, but as the money rolled in… I didn't want anything big and ostentatious, just a cute little bungalow with a nice yard, in a nice area."

"I guess that would have been nice. So what happened then?"

Sam shrugged. "The minute we got back here, your dad went out and paid the rounds for his buddies. Then there were the late night poker games and of course the casino. I think there may have even been a few women involved in his escapades. Anyway, within two months there was nothing left; not even enough to pay the next month's rent. For all that work, we were back to square one."

A long lingering silence hung over them.

"Is that why I don't really remember much about him? I don't ever remember opening Christmas presents with him, or going to a ballgame or the park."

"He was relatively good with those things when you guys were really young, but before you turned five he'd lost interest in playing the daddy role. For the next few Christmases, he promised to be there, but would either arrive hours after you guys had opened your presents and gone to bed, or worse still, he'd arrive early but he'd be so drunk, he'd ruin everything for everyone."

She threw a few things into the suitcase then ran her fingers through her hair.

"I'm sorry. I didn't mean to bring up…" She turned her attention to packing her own things.

"That's okay. It's probably time you knew a bit more about him anyway. You're a grown woman now. It's only normal that you wonder about him, but I have to admit, it's no walk through the park talking about it."

"He hurt you, didn't he?" Taryn pulled a few things out of the suitcase and when her mom didn't answer, she turned to hug her.

For a brief moment of weakness, Sam leaned into her daughter and gave way to the pain of the past.

"The important thing is," she said as she pulled back, "I got back on my feet and came out stronger than ever. I never wanted you kids to feel the effect of an absent father."

"You succeeded, Mom. And I'm sure Bobby would agree."

Sam patted Taryn's cheek. "Now enough of this talk and let's get you off to Paris."

Tar looked at the almost full suitcase and reached in to pull a few more things out. "I think I have more than enough. I'm only going for the weekend."

As she started to pull items out, Sam grabbed her wrist and stopped her.

"Bring more. You never know."

"Mom, I'm not going to leave you alone for an entire week. Bobby is so preoccupied with school. He's become so ambitious lately and all he thinks about is developing new ideas, and new recipes. I would hate to see him have to take time out from his classes to be here because you're alone."

"I told you sweetie, I'm back on my feet. I'm back to my old self. Bobby can go to his classes, work on his recipes and plan his future all he wants. In fact, I want him to. I think he's going to make a great chef one day."

Taryn grinned. "I think so, too. Who knows? Maybe one day he'll even come to the Culinary Institute in Paris."

"Can't say I wouldn't like to have an Errol King in the family," Sam said with an amused giggle. "He has all the makings to give Errol a run for his money. I just don't want the restaurant to hold him back. Sam's is my baby and I'll handle it. Bobby is smart enough to end up in Harvard or Oxford, if he chooses, and I'd rather see him there than wasting his days in my little restaurant."

"You're right. He can go as far as his imagination takes him, but still…"

"Honey, did you ever stop to consider… maybe I'd like to take care of things on my own after being on my back for so long?"

Stunned, Taryn looked at her mother.

"I'm eager to get back to Sam's. I'm eager to have those long and tiresome days that leave me exhausted, but so satisfied. And with Errol's crew… what a dream."

"If you're sure."

"Sweetie, if I see you walk through that door before the week is over, I'm going to spin you around and send you right back out."

An immense weight was lifted off Taryn's shoulder and her lungs filled with sweet and fresh air like it hadn't in a long while. Her mother's push out the door was exactly what she needed.

She clipped her suitcase shut, took a quick shower and grabbed her passport and purse.

"Take care of that man of yours, honey," Sam called from the door.

"And you take care of yourself."

"I will. Now scoot."

With a giggle and a skip in her step, Taryn hurried out to grab a cab to the airport. Once on the plane, however, she was dogged with uncertainty and questions. While her mother had made it clear she approved of Errol, Taryn couldn't help but wonder if she'd be able to keep his demons at bay. They'd been so present when she'd first met him in Paris, so much so, she'd feared staying with him could destroy her.

But now she wondered; were his demons really gone, or were they simply dormant, just waiting for the opportunity to come back?

And when they did come back, could she handle them?

# Chapter 3

Taryn was a jittery pack of nerves as she arrived at the television studios in Paris. Seeing Errol again after two weeks of aching for him, hungering for him, and dreaming of being in his arms, she wondered if she'd be able to keep from jumping all over him. This was his professional stage, after all, and she didn't want to look the fool in front of his crew.

With a broad smile on her face she reached the kitchen set where they taped his show. A clean-up crew was busy washing dishes, wiping off counters and occasionally picking in the platter of appetizing *croque monsieurs* set in a platter.

"*Pardonnez-moi*," she said in a halting accent.

Three sets of bright, brown eyes turned to her.

"*Oui*," the smaller woman said.

"Where is Errol King?"

"Errol?" She turned to the taller woman and the young man cleaning the kitchen with her. "*Est-ce qu'il est toujours ici*?"

The only word Taryn picked up was '*ici*', 'here'. Could he be gone already?

Three sets of shoulders shrugged as they looked apologetically at her.

"*Monsieur King a presque fini pour aujourd'hui.* Heez almost finish for today."

Taryn turned to the sound of the booming male voice.

"I'm the stage manager, so my eyes are everywhere, all the time," he said with a strong French accent. He walked up to her carrying a tray laden with various ingredients. "He is in his dressing room getting ready for the next taping."

"Thank you," Taryn said looking around for a clue as to where that would be.

"Just down the hall." He jutted his chin out to the right. "It's the first door on the right."

"Thanks."

She walked down the hall, eager to surprise him, but as she approached his door, she heard his voice.

"I told them to rebuild it just as it was," he said.

Taryn stepped silently closer and tried to peer into the room. The door was ajar, but all she could see was an empty sofa and the shadow of Errol pacing.

"Suzanne," he went on. "I told you, I don't want them to make any changes. La Benicoise was perfect as it was. Why change it?"

Silence.

"Okay," he said more gently. "I hadn't looked at it that way."

More silence, and Taryn realized he was on the phone.

"Yeah, I know." His voice was unusually warm and understanding. "I can't. Things are really busy here. We've been having some technical problems, so we only have four episodes in the can. Yeah, thanks, Suz. I really appreciate it."

Taryn's heart skipped a painful beat. Hearing Errol speak so intimately to Suzanne, and calling her Suz... it was all too cozy.

"Yeah. I think they're going to need a month or so before everything is set to go again."

While she understood his need to speak to his sous-chef about the progress of the rebuilding his burned down restaurant, she couldn't understand the almost loving tone he used. It was a tone she'd heard him use with her, when they were alone together, when he let his guard down, when he allowed himself to be vulnerable. She'd naively thought that tone was reserved for her, not for this vile and wicked Suzanne who hid nothing of her desire to get Errol back into her bed.

Disgusted by the conversation and the fact that Errol would have to continue to work with a woman who obviously intended to seduce him, Taryn spun around to leave. She couldn't face him like this, not when she was so distraught by what she'd heard. But her departure was brutally halted when she ran into the young stage manager.

"Ah," she cried out as she was splashed with hot coffee.

"*Ah, mon Dieu*," he said. "*Est-ce que vous allez bien*?"

The door to Errol's dressing room opened wide and Errol stepped out. "What's…? Taryn!" His smile was wide and genuine, and his eyes sexy and starving for her.

"*Je suis désolé*," the stage manager stammered, reaching out to wipe Taryn's pristine white blouse with a paper napkin. "So, so sorry. I do apologize."

"That's all right. I'm fine." She tried to pull back from his brushing hands.

In his attempts to wipe her off, he repeatedly touched her breasts. And as she glimpsed down, she could see the coffee had seeped through her blouse as well as her thin and translucent bra, leaving her nipples virtually bare.

Despite her attempt to back away, he persisted.

"Jean-Pierre, that's quite enough," Errol said.

"I did not expect her to turn around," Jean-Pierre said in defense. "Look, I ruined her blouse."

Feeling too many eyes on her breasts, Taryn blushed.

Errol reached out to physically stop Jean-Pierre's hands from groping his fiancé.

"*Ah, oui. Désolé.*" Jean-Pierre finally got his roaming hands under control.

"Jean-Pierre, this is Taryn, *ma fiancé*. She just flew in from New York."

"Ah," he said with wide and impressed eyes. "You are very lucky."

"Thank you."

"The set will be ready for the next taping in twenty-five minutes."

"I'll be there."

Jean-Pierre left them, but not before casting a final glance at Taryn's piercing nipples.

"You okay?" Errol asked. "Was the coffee hot?"

"Just very warm. I'm fine. Really. I think this blouse might be ruined, but I'm fine."

Errol's glance dipped to her coffee stained blouse. "Doesn't look all that ruined to me," he said with a wicked smile. "In fact, it looks damned fine."

She let out a heated laugh.

"Come on," he said, pulling her inside his dressing room. "You heard the man. We only have twenty-five minutes."

# Chapter 4

"I think I should go wash this off first."

"Don't worry. I'll wash you off all right. I'll lick every aromatic drop off your sumptuous breasts. Talk about *café au lait*. It'll be the best damned coffee I've ever had." He trailed his finger down her cleavage. "Oh, yeah, and sticky sweet as well. Come on. Hurry."

He tore through the buttons and peeled the dirty garment off her. Before taking off her bra, he dipped his tongue between her breasts and traced the edge of her bra with his tongue. Her breasts swelled with desire and her nipples perked up, eager for his attention. Wasting little time, he reached around, unclasped her bra and quickly filled each hand with a heavy breast. His thumbs each took possession of a nipple as he groaned his pleasure.

"Damn, I want you, Taryn." He dove between her breasts, his tongue running over one swell of her breast and quickly dipping into the valley before tasting the other. He couldn't get enough of tasting her, of holding her and sucking on her.

With brash and urgent hands, he jacked up her skirt, exposing the delicate white panty adorned with soft baby blue lace.

"Beautiful," he whispered as he wrapped his fingers around her tiny waist and sat her up on the small desk strewn with recipes, notes and lines. He pried her legs wide apart then ran a finger along the blue lace.

Taryn growled with hunger. She'd missed him, but she hadn't really realized just how much she'd needed to feel him again. Her body burned under the slightest touch.

"There's no coffee spilled down there," Taryn purred.

He leaned in closer and snaked his tongue under the thin fabric of her panty. The teasing and fleeting touch of his tongue over her clitoris had her reaching back over the desk looking for something to clutch, to hold onto. In only a matter of minutes, he'd managed to bring her on the edge of an explosive orgasm.

"Hold on, my worldly chef. You're heating me up too fast. You did say we have twenty minutes, right." She reached out to undo his pants and let them fall to his ankles.

Jumping off the desk, she pushed him back until he was backed to the wall. "Do I have to wait until someone spills coffee on you before I can taste you?"

Errol yanked his underwear off and held his erection out to her. "Absolutely not."

With the limited time they had, she wanted to drive him as crazy as she could. She lightly ran her fingers over the length of him, amused by the spontaneous movement of his arousal her touch brought.

Lacking any degree of patience, he pressed her fingers around his rigid shaft and purposefully pumped her hand over his erection.

"I'll take the time to slowly savor you tonight, but for now…" He spun her around, pinned her to the wall and forcefully pushed his raging erection into her, a loud grunt of euphoria filling the air as her heated body took him in.

The walls shook under the weight of their movements. Meeting up with Errol again was even more powerful than she'd imagined. His touch easily fanned the embers that had lain in wait since his departure. Every inch of her body tingled with joy, burned with hunger and yearned for more and more.

He passionately clamped his lips over hers, drinking her in, breathing her in, his very hunger for her arousing her all the more. His lips trailed down her neck, and behind her ear.

"Look what you do to me," he whispered in a husky voice. "You make me feel like an innocent and virginal boy who's never touched a woman before. You excite me to the point that nothing else exists."

And with those words, he pounded into her, grunting with every push, a grunt that was echoed with her own erotic cries of ecstasy.

For a long sated moment, only their heaving breaths filled the air.

"Damn, I love your sweet ass, Taryn." He leaned his sweaty brow against hers and met her gaze.

Smiling, she ran the back of her hand down his cheek. "I think you have about ten minutes left to make yourself look presentable before heading back out there."

He captured her lips in a deep and loving kiss before backing away. "Maybe now I'll be better able to concentrate on the work at hand. Being away from you has left me a little absent minded lately."

"Well, I'm glad I could come over and help you out." She smiled naughtily at him.

Running his hand through his luxurious hair, he gazed at the mirror, grinned then quickly changed clothes. "I guess a fresh shirt wouldn't hurt. I'll pull one out for you, too."

Minutes later they walked out and headed to the set. While Errol was greeted with cordial professionalism and quickly escorted to his station, Taryn couldn't help but notice the knowing smiles that spread over the faces of the crew as they gazed at her.

She was suddenly all too aware of her messed up hair and Errol's shirt on her back.

# Chapter 5

Six hours later, they called it a wrap.

"All that time and you've only taped two half hour shows?" Taryn said to Errol as he walked off set and came to her.

"I think you're more of a distraction than I'd anticipated." He led her back to his dressing room. "Instead of seeing the chicken breasts in front of me, all I could see were yours in my face. And when I had to whip some cream, I couldn't help but think about the next time I'd be able to have you at my mercy. And I just about lost it when I had to open those oysters. Damn, but all I could think of was shoving my tongue over your clitoris and hearing your squeal."

Leaning against the doorjamb, she watched him shun his white shirt lightly dusted with flour and change into a pristine blue shirt. "Am I to understand that you're blaming your inability to tape more than one half hour's worth of material in three hours on me?"

He chuckled, buttoned up his shirt and took her by the elbow. "Come on. I don't want thoughts of fucking you keep me from catching up tomorrow. I have big plans for the night."

With a giggle she followed him out of the studio to his car in the parking lot. Driving home was like a brief promenade down memory lane. All the architecture that had impressed her on her arrival to Paris that very first time; the Eiffel Tower in the distance, le Louvre and Notre-Dame de Paris. She hadn't realized just how much she'd missed everything about Paris.

Minutes later they pulled up to his place and Taryn felt a strong sense of being home the moment he opened the door to his place.

"Welcome home, *mon amour*."

Lost in the moment, Taryn kicked off her shoes and hurried to the large windows in the living area. The view had always made her spirits soar and, as she pulled back the drapes, she was once again swept away by the magnificent view of the city.

"Paris shines bright once more, now that you're here with me." Errol came up behind her and wrapped his arms around her waist.

Letting out a lighthearted laugh, she leaned back into him and felt more at home than she had in a long while. "I never want to tear my eyes off it, it's so beautiful."

"The city of lights. It never fails to move me."

Moved by the romanticism, Taryn wanted to stay wrapped in his arms a few moments more. "It feels so good to be home," she whispered. "I have so many memories of this place."

"So do I," he groaned from deep in his throat. "So much so, I think I'm going to cancel tomorrow's taping. I think I need a few days off."

All of Paris offered so many memories; her first encounter with Errol, his invitation to become his plaything, her initiation to the kind of sex she'd never imagined herself involved in. She'd been such a bundle of naïve nerves, so unsure of herself, and so mesmerized by Errol; his handsome face, his sexy body, and his charm.

"It feels good having you home." He lightly tapped her butt. "I'll go get us a glass of wine."

She tore her eyes off the lights of the city and watched Errol head to the kitchen. The apartment was the same as she remembered. Masculine, strong, rich and sexy, just like the man of the house.

Following Errol, she entered the dining room and was suddenly gripped with an unexpected sense of dread and gloom. The dining room table…

"Red good?" Errol called from the kitchen.

"Sure," Taryn muttered. Her skin tingled, but not for the same reasons it had tingled just moments before.

From a distance she heard the subtle pop of a cork being pulled out of a bottle, the gentle clink of wine glasses coming out of the cupboard and the soft swish of rich red wine filling a glass then another. She was barely conscious of Errol's approaching footsteps.

"Here you go."

He held the glass out in front of her, but she just stared straight ahead.

"Taryn?"

His light touch on her shoulder registered, but she still couldn't bring herself to answer him.

"Are you okay?"

She nodded then shook her head. "That's where…" She leaned against the back of a chair.

"Taryn, what's wrong?"

She shivered as her heart began pounding faster and louder while the walls slowly caved into her. All she could hear was her heart beating loudly and her breath becoming shorter and shorter. Gripped with a sudden fear and panic, Taryn wrapped her arms around herself trying to stop her shivering, while sweat beaded up on her temples.

"Are you cold, honey? You're shivering."

"I think I need to go."

"What are you talking about? We just got here. The flight over here must be getting to you. You just need to relax a bit."

"I can't stay here, Errol. I…"

"What's going on?" He set the wine glasses on the table and took her hand.

"This is where… Errol… that night, when you tied me up and left me…"

"Oh, Taryn." He pulled her into his arms and held her tight. "I'm so sorry about that night."

"It took me so long to forget about that night. It was weeks before I finally stopped having nightmares. I'd put it all out of my head. I'd gotten over it and have forgotten all about that horrible night. But now… staring at the very table you'd tied me to and left me… in the dark."

"I'll never let anything like that happen again. You'll see. There's nothing to be afraid of."

"I know, Errol, but…"

"Okay, let's head back into the living area then. I swear, first thing tomorrow I have this damned table thrown into the fire and I'll get a new table, a virgin table."

"No. I can't stay here, Errol." She brought her trembling hand to her throat and tugged at the collar of the shirt Errol had loaned her. "I have to get out of here. I can't breathe."

She tore free of his hold and stormed to the door of his apartment.

"Taryn, wait."

"I can't Errol. I don't want to be left in the dark, Errol. I can't. Anything, but I can't stay in the dark. I'll be good, Errol, I promise. I don't want to be tied up in the dark. Never. Never again."

Shocked by her fear, Errol put a hand to her shoulder. "Never, Taryn. I'll never leave you in the dark again."

The very air in the apartment choked her. The apartment that had captivated her just moments earlier was now a painful reminder of that night of hell. She'd never been at ease in the dark, and the fear had grown over the years, but that night… tied up, unable to move, unable to see. It was her worst nightmare. Her breath came in short, sharp pants that hurt her lungs and stung the back of her throat. She'd throw up if she stayed any longer… as sure as she was standing there, she'd throw up right on him.

She turned the doorknob, but neglected to unlock the deadbolt, keeping her from opening the door and adding to her panic. "I want to get out," she shouted as she pounded on the door. "I have to get out."

Errol grabbed her and threw his arms around her. "Okay," he whispered. "Okay, we'll go. There are hundreds of hotels we can go to." He turned the lock and opened the door. "We'll go somewhere else, Taryn. Anywhere else."

The moment she stepped into the corridor she calmed down.

"Stay here," he said. "I'm going to go back in, grab a few things and we'll be out of here in no time, okay?"

She nodded and immediately realized how ridiculous she was being, but was unable to stop herself. The apartment she'd looked forward to returning to was now just one big, horrible memory.

# Chapter 6

After a sleepless night in a beautiful hotel room, Taryn turned to Errol's sleeping form and stared at him. She could hardly believe he'd so easily given in to her outlandish demand. How could she possibly ask him to leave his home, his magnificent apartment? Shaking off the last shivers left by her panic attack of the night before and the dream filled night that had left her trembling more than once, she got out of bed and switched on the coffee machine set on the little breakfast table. As it percolated, she opened the door to collect the fragrant breakfast basket left in the hall.

Just as the rich aroma of coffee filled the air and blended with the fresh scent of croissants and real butter, Errol's eyes fluttered open. In an instant he was propped up on his elbows, his concerned eyes riveted to her.

"Are you okay?"

"I'm fine," she said with a bit of a nervous laugh. She set the basket by the coffee machine. "Coffee?"

He dared a slight smile as he sat up and nodded.

"I'm terribly sorry about last night." She poured coffee into two cups and brought him one.

"There's nothing to be sorry about, Taryn."

She returned to the basket, generously buttered two croissants and set them on a plate accompanied by a tiny cup of strawberry jam. "It was silly and childish of me." She handed him his breakfast. "Your apartment is wonderful and I love the view and… I can't believe I made you bring me out to a hotel. I'm past all that silliness now. After breakfast we can go back."

"*Merci, ma chérie.*" He took the plate and tore off a large chunk. "You really think one night's sleep will have washed away everything that frightened you so much last night?"

She nodded as she reached for her croissant.

He shook his head. "I don't believe you. You're trying to be strong, and I appreciate it, but I really think you need more time away from the apartment."

"But I have been away, Errol… for months."

"Well, then maybe I'll just have to consider selling the apartment." He smiled and cupped her cheek. "It was growing too small anyway."

Touched by his words and his actions, Taryn smiled as her eyes filled with emotional tears while she kissed him. “What do you propose we do? Stay in this hotel until you sell it?”

“Not quite. Finish up. I have something to show you.”

An hour later they were blinded by the morning sun as they drove over rolling hills, through lush fields and past the most adorable little houses she’d ever seen. It was a postcard perfect landscape everywhere she looked.

“Can you at least give me a hint of where you’re taking me?”

“It’s beautiful.”

She gazed at the charming countryside. “Well, that narrows it down.”

“It’s peaceful.”

Looking up at the sun, she tried to figure out what direction they were driving in, but it was nearly noon and with all the twists and turns, it was hard to determine which way they were going.

“Okay, I’ll give you a final hint. It’s a place I love to go to when I need to lose myself, or find myself, depending on how you want to look at it. It’s a place that has everything I need, everything I want and it never fails to lift my spirits."

Gasping she turned to look at him. "Are you taking me to your childhood home?"

He smiled as he turned onto a narrow winding road. "It's just a little farmhouse I bought for Nana a while back. It's close to the village where she raised me, so I knew she'd feel at home there and I had it equipped with every conceivable modern convenience you can think of. She loved it. Of course you can't have a farmhouse without having acres and acres of land, and the fields that surround the house are about as fertile as they come."

"That's very generous of you. Your Nana must have really appreciated it."

Letting out an amused snort, he slowed the car down as more and more homes lined the narrow street. Soon they passed a few businesses. "It's nothing compared to everything she's given me over the years."

He slowed down as they arrived in the heart of the small village. "It might be a good idea to stop for previsions. I called late last night to make sure the house was in livable condition, but I doubt they had time to adequately fill the refrigerator."

Parking the car in front of a line of small shops, he grabbed her hand and brought it to his lips. "Come. I want to introduce you to my childhood."

Beaming, she got out of the car and followed him to the entrance of a pastry shop. "The pastry here is fabulous. Even I can't top it."

"I find that hard to believe."

The tinkling of the bell above the door announced their entry. Immediately Taryn was assaulted by the heavenly scent of sweet pastries, buttery croissants and delectable tarts.

"*Bonjour, je peux vous aider?*" a young woman called from behind the counter.

"This is where I tasted my first cream puff," Errol said as he approached her. "*Quatre petits choux, s'il vous plait,*" he ordered as he held up four fingers.

As the woman placed the four cream puffs in a small white box and tied it with string, Errol said, "Wait until you taste these. You'll think you've died and gone to heaven."

"*Voila*," the woman said.

Errol paid for the pastries. "*Merci*."

Their next stop was the butcher shop.

"I was barely eight years old when I came to this *boucherie* every week to pick up Nana's favorite cuts of beef. By the time I was twelve I knew every cut there was; every cut of beef, pork, chicken, lamb, you name it."

An older man with a blood stained apron came out from the cold room in the back.

"*Eh, bien. Si ce n'est pas le beau Errol,*" the old man exclaimed with a friendly smile.

"*Armand, quelle plaisir.*" With his hand set delicately at the small of her back, he brought Taryn forward. "Taryn, this is Armand Descoteaux, the very man who taught me everything I know about meat."

Armand smiled as he reached over the counter to shake her hand. "*Bonjour, mademoiselle.*"

"*Je pourrais avoir un filet de porc et une demi-livre de foie gras*?"

"*Bien sur. Mais tu vas faire attention au chien, n'est-ce pas?*"

Errol laughed along with Armand, a loud, boyish and almost silly laugh. Taryn had never seen him so carefree, so unabashedly happy.

"When I was ten, Nana sent me to get a very special order," Errol explained. "Armand had this huge roast all wrapped up and I had tied it to the rack on the back of my bike. As I drove off I felt a light tug and almost lost my balance, but I managed to get control, didn't bother looking back and rode off. I only had time to ride a few feet away when Armand came out calling after me." With tears of amusement in his eyes, Errol glanced at Armand before going on. "*Noireau*, this black mutt who lived next door, had sniffed out my roast and had managed to pull it off my bike rack before I could take off. I ran around the block twice trying to catch that damn thing."

"Your Nana must not have been amused," Taryn said with a smile.

Errol reached over the counter and affectionately patted Armand's arm. "This man saved me from Nana's wrath. Had I arrived without her roast and without the francs she'd given me… well, suffice it to say Armand got me out of a tight spot."

"And, he pay me back many times over," the man said in stilted English.

Moments later, with his bundles of meat wrapped up in butcher paper, Errol called, "*Au revoir*," over his shoulder and they headed to their next stop.

"You really have a special bond with the people of this village, don't you?" Taryn remarked as they walked out.

"A lifetime of memories with people who really had a hand in making me the man I am today."

Taryn nodded. "It takes a village…"

"Yes," Errol agreed. "And thank goodness they helped Nana raise me. I was quite a handful."

After a few more purchases, a baguette, a wheel of cheese and a few choice bottles of wine, they got back in the car. Only five minutes later, Errol pulled onto a gravel road.

As the car came to a rolling stop, Taryn looked in front of them as the most beautiful home came into view. The large wooden structure was rustic and charming, but far from being the little farmhouse Errol has led her to believe. The two-story home could easily house a huge family and then some.

"You should have seen it when I first bought it. Really run down. But I had those boards sanded down and tinted, threw on a few shutters here and there, and just enough gingerbread to give it that delicate touch."

"It's breathtaking, Errol. All the flowers, all the warmth…" Every window had a flower box filled with tiny blue, pink and white flowers. Flanking the front door were two half barrels overflowing with larger flowers of the same colors.

"Wait until you see inside." He hopped out of the car, rummaged through his pocket and pulled out an old fashioned key.

Tickled and eager to see the home he so obviously loved, Taryn followed close behind.

"Ladies first," he said as he pushed open the door.

Taryn stepped into a house that screamed of another era. Wide planks of rough wood made up the floor and the steps leading to the second floor were roughly honed out of solid wood. The walls were littered with wrought iron sconces and the railing of the stairs was also in the same heavy black metal. It boasted charm in every corner.

"Come on," Errol said, beaming from ear to ear. "I'll show you around."

Enthused by his boyish good humor, Taryn tucked her arm under his and followed him to the living room. A large and colorful throw rug covered much of the hardwood floor and bushels of yellow flowers were tucked away in every corner. Fanciful paintings adorned the walls and a large ceramic cat lay on the coffee table.

The kitchen, rustic and charming with its old world blue and white ceramic tile, large porcelain sink with retro faucets and old fashioned lighting fixtures was equipped with a double refrigerator, a cooking range with six heating elements, two regular ovens, a wide bread and pizza oven, microwave and convection oven and a thermal cooker.

"Wow. You really didn't hold back, did you?"

"I told you it was well equipped. Nana loved to cook and I wanted to make sure everything she did was enjoyable." He opened a cupboard that housed every conceivable cooking apparatus any cook could dream of. "If she wanted to make pastries, she had a mixer for the dough. If she wanted to make pasta of any kind, she had the pasta maker. If she was a milkshake or a smoothie, she had the blender. And everything in between."

"I'm already looking forward to cooking."

"Down here we have a small bathroom, and…" He turned onto the steps that led upstairs. "Up here we have…"

Taryn came up behind him and was surprised by the immensity of the bedroom. It virtually took up the whole floor.

"Over there," he said, pointing to the far right, "is the master bathroom, complete with therapeutic bath, shower, bidet, and his and hers sinks… no arguing over space in the morning."

"But what about your Nana? Where did she sleep?"

Errol let out a chuckle. "I only recently had the second floor redone. On the one hand I wanted the added space, on the other, it was always painful for me to pass in front of Nana's room knowing she wasn't here anymore. Seeing her in the kitchen, or out in the gardens was one thing, but seeing her up in her room, lying in her bed… those last few weeks as she slowly ebbed away."

"It certainly is an impressive room."

A huge, four-poster, king-sized bed took center stage. Several large paintings, abstract nudes and stylized love scenes, filled the walls.

"It's a complete turnaround from what it was when Nana lived here. This is the one place that doesn't resemble her at all." His smile was suddenly sad.

Taryn put her hand to his shoulder. "Why don't you bring me out to the gardens, then."

With a sad, reminiscing smile, he nodded.

The gardens, though in serious need of tender loving care, were expansive and varied. Beautiful flowers bloomed in a variety of colors and sizes. Sumptuous roses, playful black-eyed Susans and gigantic sunflowers thrived despite the neglect.

"I have workers come every once in a while to help out in the fields." He pointed to the fields far beyond the garden. "But I guess they've neglected the flower garden a bit."

"Just a few weeds growing here and there. It wouldn't take much work to get it looking as beautiful as when your Nana tended to it."

Errol shot her a sidelong glance. "I was afraid you might not like it out here."

"Really? What's not to like? It's pure heaven, Errol. Why would you think such a thing?"

He shrugged. "You're a big city girl… from New York, the city that never sleeps, and you came to Paris, the city of lights. This is a far cry from the excitement and thrill of either."

"You're all the excitement and thrill I need." She turned to him and brushed her fingers along his unshaven cheek. "I love it, Errol. I'm already looking forward to cooking in that fabulous kitchen, and look at some of these fresh vegetables." She roamed through the rows of growing vegetables. "Even if the garden has been neglected a bit, look at these gorgeous tomatoes, and these leeks, and, oh, look at all these snow peas."

She snapped one off the plant and took a bite. "You can never find anything this fresh in Paris. I mean, this is literally straight off the vine." She held out the remainder for him to taste.

Taking a bite, Errol went on to nibble on her fingers until she giggled. "I'm so happy you like it." He leaned in and lightly kissed her. "When I initially bought this for Nana, I had it decorated and remodeled to suit her needs, but also her personality. This is a house for a strong and beautiful woman. A woman who knows how to handle a wild boy…" He eyed her knowingly.

"Are you referring to me?"

"Nana managed to control the rebellious boy. You managed the impossible. You tamed the wild man… the man who definitely did not want to be tamed. But here we are. You took that wild man and turned him into a better person, a stronger man."

"I am flattered that you would put me up beside your Nana."

"And Nana would be proud to stand beside you."

"You think so?"

"I have no doubt." He kissed the tip of her nose and gave her an affectionate pat on the butt. "Stroll through the garden, or get acquainted with the kitchen, or whatever you like. I'll go get the luggage out of the car and start our dinner."

The moment he returned with their dinner, Taryn joined him in the kitchen and they set to work. In addition to the pork he'd bought, Tar brought in leeks, tomatoes, red peppers and several zucchinis. Like a well-oiled machine they worked efficiently, in sync, and with a few stolen kisses here and there. While he took care of the pork and the *foie gras*, she chopped vegetables and stir fried them.

When the meal was ready half an hour later, Taryn gladly sat down to the meal.

"I hadn't realized just how hungry I was."

"It has been a long day." He speared his fork into his *foie gras*. "Eat up," he urged. "I have a big night planned for you."

She smiled as she eyed him. "I bet it's nothing compared to what I have planned for you."

# Chapter 7

An empty bottle of wine lay on the table and their dinner plates had virtually been licked clean. As Errol licked the remainder of his cream puff off his fingers of, Taryn reached for his hand and brought the sweet digit to her mouth.

"I'm still hungry," she groaned.

"I apologize for not offering. How rude of me."

"I think I'm going to have to find a way for you to make it up to me."

He playfully pushed the white pastry box containing the two remaining cream puffs to her. "You can always take another entire pastry."

"That's not really what I had in mind." She stood and gazed at him with the silent demand he do the same. Still holding his finger, she led him out of the kitchen and up the stairs.

"I don't think there's any food stashed up here."

"I'm sure we'll find another way for you to appease my appetite."

In his huge room, she pushed him to the wall, unbuckled his belt and whipped it off. "I suggest you be a good boy from now on, Errol."

"Yes, Taryn."

With slow and patient motions, she unzipped his pants and let them fall to his bare feet. With a commanding tap on one calf then the other, she had him lift his foot in order to get the pants out of her way.

With the same unhurried motions she prepared to rid him of his tight, white boxer briefs. "As beautiful as these are on you, the way they mold perfectly to you," she said as she ran a finger over the length of his growing erection, "I think I prefer you without them."

"If you must," Errol said.

She pulled them off and flung them across the room. As if looking for something in particular, she examined his hard-on.

"Do you think it might appease your appetite?"

"I'm not sure." She held his erection up to her mouth. "Let's have a taste."

She lightly licked the tip of his hard-on and Errol quickly responded with a thrilled groan.

"Taste some more."

She ran her tongue over the length of his shaft and leaned back. "Hmm, I'm not sure."

"Try again."

With a skeptic glance up at him, she brought his entire length into her mouth and lightly sucked.

"Yeah," he whispered as he shoved his fingers through her hair and pulled her to him. "You like that?"

For a few tantalizing moments she sucked on him, reveling in the taste of him, until she saw his toes roll up and tasted the salty result of her sucking, the precursor to his full, climactic spillage. Without warning, she let him go, stood and walked away.

"No," she said, hiding an amused smile. "I don't think that will do." When she reached the door to the bathroom, she turned back to look at him. "I'm in the mood for something else."

Stunned and extremely horny, Errol leaned against the wall, his eyes wide with disbelief. "You can't just leave me like this."

"I just did," she called from the bathroom. She closed the door. "I just realized I didn't shower this morning."

Smiling behind the closed door, she heard Errol's pounding footsteps quickly approach as she stripped her clothes off. She hurried to hop in the shower before he opened the door.

"Now that you mention it, I didn't shower this morning either."

"I'll only be a minute then it's all yours," Taryn teased.

He tore the door to the shower stall open. "I think it's time I take what's mine," he said in a deep and highly aroused voice, before crushing her to him.

# Chapter 8

Taryn was already aroused as she stirred to wakefulness. Her night with Errol should have completely sated her, but she found her body craving him again. Her skin still tingled with his heated touch, and her nipples were proof of the effect he had on her, even when he no longer touched her.

Licking her lips, she remembered his hungry kisses as his hands had roamed over her wet and soapy body. He had wasted little time jumping into the shower with her. Though she'd tried to maintain control and keep the upper hand, she'd quickly succumbed to his kisses, and when he pressed the length of his body against hers, there was no turning back.

Within the tight confines of the shower stall they'd tasted each other's body, wet, sleek and fresh. When she exploded under the strong wave of her orgasm, she'd expected Errol to release his pent up passion, but instead, he'd carried her to his bed and had slowly and tenderly made love to her.

She smiled as the expression on his face in the moment's preceding his climax came to her. The blend of ultimate arousal and profound love had brought her to a height of euphoria she'd never dreamed of.

A constant and persistent pounding pierced through her reverie and she cracked an eye open.

"Sorry about the racket," Errol said.

Taryn sat up to look at him. Wearing only his drawstring pajama pants he was a beautiful sight. His toned torso had a pleasant golden glow that immediately beckoned her hands for a touch. And she couldn't ignore his abs, well defined without being obnoxiously sculpted, they led her eyes down to the crux of his thighs where a light sprinkling of hair growth was visible.

"What are you doing out of bed so early?" she said as her eyes continued to drink him in.

He tilted his head to the window, acknowledging the noise coming from outside.

"What is that?"

"The farmhands. I'm surprised you didn't wake up earlier. They've been at it since the crack of dawn. Some of the crops are ready for harvest and there's no time to waste."

Taryn got out of bed and headed to the window. In the distance, several men worked the fields.

"What do you grow?"

"Corn, a bit of barley and where they are now is potatoes."

The pounding she heard were the first potatoes thrown into a stainless steel barrel.

"They should be finished in a few hours. When the sun gets too high, it gets way too hot to work. That's why they're here so early."

"This is really an impressive piece of land you have here. I didn't realize yesterday just how big it was."

"Get dressed. We'll have breakfast and go out to see it all from close up."

She threw on a pretty flowing summer dress. Splashed with fragile yellow flowers, the white dress was cut modestly in the front, but more daringly in the back. The spaghetti straps were tied in a bow on each shoulder.

"What a pretty frock. It almost seems as if you packed it especially for the open air and countryside."

Pleased with his reaction, she followed him down the stairs.

"What smells so heavenly?"

"Blueberry crepes with custard and brown sugar."

Taryn ate three whole crepes downed with good strong coffee. "What a perfect way to start the day."

"Now that I've filled your belly, let's go see if the guys have finished yet."

As they walked out, many of the men were leaving the field and boarding a large pickup truck. In the back, bushels of potatoes were lined front to back.

"Looks like they've had a healthy harvest. Come on. I'll show you the other fields."

They strolled past tall stalks of corn, windswept strands of barley and finally came to a portion of the land that was not visible from the house.

"A vineyard?"

Errol beamed. "It's the crowning jewel."

Rows upon rows of grapevines ran off as far as the eye could see.

"What's a country home in France without your own vineyard?" He reached for a heavy bunch of deep blue grapes. "If all goes well, I should have my own merlot out soon."

"Are they good to eat?"

In response, Errol pulled a bunch off the vine and held it over her head so she could pluck off a grape with her teeth.

"Umm," she moaned with a nod.

"Imagine once they've fermented into the perfect wine." He glanced at the nearby vines, then at her. With a mischievous grin, he opened a small tool shed a few yards away at the head of the rows, pulled out two cutters and several flat bottomed baskets. "Come on. Let's grab a few and see what we can do."

"Now?" she said with an amused grin.

"Why not?" He quickly clipped bunch after bunch and placed them in the basket

Eager to do her part, Tar took the cutters and snipped off several bunches. With their baskets full, he led her back to the tool shed. With a twinkle in his eye, he pulled open a wide sliding door that exposed a large wooden vat.

"Let's try it the old fashioned way."

"Are you nuts?" She burst out laughing.

Unperturbed, Errol plopped the grapes off each bunch and tossed them in. Tickled by the thought, Taryn slipped out of her sandals.

"Ladies first." Errol held her dainty hand and helped her in.

The grapes squished between her toes in a strange and interesting way. "This tickles."

Errol dug his hands into the grapes, squeezing them between his fingers while the juices ran down his arms.

"I don't think wine will ever taste the same after this." He rubbed his juiced up hands up her calf.

"Errol!" she shrieked. "You're going to stain my dress."

"Then I strongly suggest you take it off," he said as his hands drove up to her thighs.

She pulled the skirt of her dress up and he gripped her bare ass cheeks, leaving bright blue hand prints on her white skin. With a giggle, she pulled the dress over her head and set it on the nearby fence post just as Errol's hands traveled over her belly and up to her bare breasts.

"Keep working your feet in those grapes if you ever want to taste my world famous merlot."

He wrapped his hands around her waist and leaned in to lick the grape juice that now trickled over her breasts. Her nipples perked to attention.

"This isn't fair," she moaned. "I'm a mess and you're pristine."

"There's hardly room in there for two." He pointed his chin to the vat.

"I'll make room." She backed up and tugged on his hand. "There's plenty of room. We could lie down in here."

He pulled his drawstring pajamas off and got in.

Taryn immediately pressed her breasts to his chest, crushing more grapes between them. Hungry to taste more of him, she tilted her head up to kiss him. His lips crushed over hers while his tongue played wicked games in her mouth. With grapes between his fingers, he ran his hands over her face, and through her hair. As his body slithered against hers, his erection poked and prodded here and there, heightening her arousal.

"I have an idea for a very original, very personalized wine." He wrapped his arms around her waist and picked her up, bringing her legs around his hips to straddle him. "Like you said, there's enough room to lie down in here."

He set her down in the grapes, pried her legs open then squeezed a handful of grapes over her clitoris.

Staring up at him, she licked her lips in anticipation. "I have a feeling I'm going to really like this wine."

Errol bent over her and looked at her crotch. "So am I." He ran his tongue thoroughly over all the juices that trickled down from her clitoris and covered the sensitive and fragile flesh that hungered for even more of his touch.

"Oh, please don't stop," she groaned when he removed his tongue.

"This is so sweet, I don't think I could stop even if I wanted to."

Setting his entire mouth over her, clamping his lips over her nether lips, he lick and bit her to the edge of an exquisite orgasm, but he stopped just short of giving her that pleasure.

"Not yet, baby," he whispered. He tugged her up and turned her over, setting her on her knees, her back to him. Grape juice ran down her back as he slid his erection between her thighs. "I want to savor this sweet wine."

Taking a firm hold of her breasts, he squeezed the firm flesh, and tweaked her nipples. A tortured moan of unbearable pleasure slipped between Taryn's lips.

"Errol," she whispered. "I want to feel you."

He nudged his hard-on against the moist opening that awaited him. "You feel that?"

"Not enough."

He nudged in a bit deeper. "How's that?"

She smiled. While she enjoyed the game of long and torturous foreplay, she thought it'd also be fun to turn the tables. "Yes, that's good."

Errol remained silent for a long stunned moment. "Maybe a little more."

"No," she snapped, pulling away suddenly. "That's enough just like that." Swinging her hips back and forth, she lightly played over the tip of Errol's erection. Biting back a smile, she said, "Just like that… that's real nice."

More stunned silence.

"Yeah," she groaned as she pushed over him just a little bit more. "That's real nice."

"Don't you want it all?"

"This is perfect." As she continued the half play over his shaft, she heard his distinct frustration as he exhaled a long, slow breath.

"The hell it is," Errol finally growled. He dug his fingers into her hips, took a firm grip and roughly pulled her to him as he plowed his engorged shaft in deep as far as it would go. "Tell me how you like that now."

No words came to her. No words could describe how she felt; how he made her feel. All that came past her lips was an animal groan that begged for more.

# Chapter 9

"I think it's time we start considering returning to Paris," Tar said as she stirred her coffee. They'd been up for all of fifteen minutes and she'd been looking for the best way to bring the topic up. In the end, she decided to just come out with it.

"Why? Don't you like it here?" Errol flipped a few fluffy pancakes onto a plate. The whole house smelled cozy, warm, sweet.

"I love it, but I do have a restaurant I have to tend to, remember?" She dropped a handful of blueberries over the pancakes and poured thick, dark maple syrup over it all. Running her finger over the lip of the syrup bottle, she cleaned off the stray drop of sweet liquid and licked her delicious finger.

He cocked his head to the side and furrowed his brow. "You want to go back to New York?"

"Errol, you knew I was just coming out to see you only for the weekend. I have responsibilities back home."

"I realize that, but I thought… what with my crew at your restaurant, and didn't you say your mom was back on her feet? What's the rush? I've been getting word from Brent back home that things are going very well. They've grown accustomed to the menu at Sam's and they're very comfortable working there. What's the problem?"

"The problem is that my mother is just barely back on her feet. She went back to the restaurant for the first time yesterday. With Bobby still caught up in his classes, and spending all his free time working on his own recipes, he won't be around to help her out. Despite the help of your crew there are still a lot of other things to tend to… like all the paper work, ordering food, preparing advertisements. I don't want her to over exert herself. I don't want her to do it all by herself."

"Tar, these past two weeks have been hell for me. Haven't they been hell for you?"

"Sure they have, but I try to call you as often as I can."

"And I appreciate that, but it's not like having you here. I mean, the phone sex is great and I love the sound of your sexy voice… you always turn me on and it doesn't take long, but… I'm not the type of man who's meant to be celibate, Tar. Your voice and my hand can only do so much."

She shot him a hard and accusing glare, but immediately softened it. "What are you trying to tell me, Errol?"

"Don't look at me like that, honey. I'm not saying anything other than I want you here, with me. I need you here, in the flesh. For crying out loud, if it wasn't for those long distance calls, I would have been flying to New York every other day. But all those calls are good for a week or two, but I don't want to go back to that… not so soon. I want you with me. You just got here. I don't get it. I thought you wanted us to be together. Why are you in such a rush to live separate lives?"

Taryn reached out to take his hand. "You know better than that, Errol. It's not that I don't want to stay here with you. This weekend has been great, more than I'd dreamed of, and I absolutely love it out here, but I can't just ignore what's waiting for me back home."

Nodding pensively, Errol took a few bites of his breakfast, took a long and loud slurp of his coffee, then set his cup down with finality. "Yesterday you sounded completely enamored with the idea of moving out here, of making France your home. How much time did we spend on the internet looking for a new apartment? I even took appointments to visit three of them and I thought you'd want to check them out with me."

Surprised and a little tickled by his attentive desire to tend to her new disdain for his apartment, she gazed at him. "You took appointments? You didn't tell me that."

"I wanted to surprise you. Of course, I didn't know you'd want to go back so soon, so I made the appointments for next week. I'll have to call to change it."

"Errol, you didn't have to do that…"

"I knew you dreaded the idea of returning to my place, so I wanted to go back to Paris and check these places out. After only a few nights in a hotel, we could be settled into a new place… just like that." He snapped his fingers.

She smiled, touched by just how quickly he'd acted on her fears. He could so simply have ignored them; pat her on the head and tell her to get over it. "That's really sweet of you, Errol. I appreciate it, really."

"Appreciate it so much you're going to just leave and return to New York?"

"Please don't make me feel guilty for doing what I feel I need to do, Errol. Think of your Nana. If she were the one at home alone and in need of you, would you just turn your back on her so you could be with me?"

He remained silent a long time then took in a long and deep breath. "Fine. After breakfast we'll head back to Paris. But will you at least humor me?"

"What do you mean?"

"At least take the time to come see the apartments with me, and then we'll…"

"And then we'll what?"

"We'll see what we'll do from there. Maybe once you see our new home you'll forget all about New York."

Not wanting to argue the matter any longer, Taryn nodded and finished her breakfast. She thought she'd made her intentions clear when she'd arrived, but evidently she hadn't.

During the long drive back to Paris, Taryn was filled with melancholia. She'd never thought of herself as a country girl, but the country air had quickly grown on her and leaving out here with Errol was something she could now very much imagine.

More than anything she longed to stay at Errol's side, whether in Paris or out here, but she wished he'd understand her need to return to New York.

As the Paris skyline rose over the horizon, and the rolling green hills fell further and further behind, her heart pounded with anticipation and trepidation. Paris was beautiful, filled with so much history and art, and it was the culinary heartbeat of the world, but New York... Her home, her heart, her love, her family. Leaving it all behind wasn't that easy.

"The first apartment overlooks the Seine," Errol said as he maneuvered through the narrow streets bordering the river. He pulled up to the impressive stone building. They met the real estate agent in the front hall and took the elevator up to the fourteenth floor.

"It has a smaller kitchen than I'm accustomed to," he discreetly said to her, "but the bedroom is impressive, and you can't beat the view."

Though her heart wasn't completely in it, Taryn followed him to the window in the bedroom. The view was indeed impressive, and while the kitchen may have been smaller than he was accustomed to, it was spacious nonetheless.

"What do you think?" he asked as he ran his hand over the window sill.

"It's very romantic… very old world. I love the woodwork and the cabinets."

At the second apartment, Taryn was impressed by the immensity of the bathroom, but the view left much to be desired. Only on the fifth floor, the best they could hope for was a glimpse of the Eiffel Tower if they pressed their face to a window.

"I thought it was on the fifteenth floor. Had I known it was the fifth, we wouldn't have bothered. Let's hope the third one is a winner," Errol said with optimism.

As soon as they pulled up to the tall building, Taryn had a feeling they'd like this one. And the moment they stepped out of the private elevator and into the enormous dwelling, her feeling was confirmed. Despite her intention to return to New York, she couldn't help but be impressed with the beautiful and spacious apartment. Ornate woodwork, intricate details, beautiful mosaic floor tiles, elegant doorknobs, majestic windows… it was more than she could have hoped for. Taking up the entire top floor of the nine story building, the three-hundred and sixty degree views were unparalleled.

"This is spectacular," she whispered to Errol. "We can see the Eiffel Tower over the Seine out of the bedroom, and there are a dozen windows in the living room that allow us to see practically to Le Louvre, and from the dining room… well, I'm sure on a clear day we could see all the way to Versailles. And then there's everything in between…"

"I think we have a winner," Errol said to the real estate agent.

"*Parfait, monsieur*," the agent replied with a pleased grin.

"Don't you think we should discuss it a bit longer," Taryn whispered as she tugged on Errol's arm. "Maybe we should sleep on in and come to a decision tomorrow."

"Why? This place is perfect. It has the space I need in the kitchen, the romance of this old world architecture you want and the view we both love. And look at that living room. We can dance in that room."

"If monsieur and madame will follow me, there is also the rooftop gardens and terrace."

Taryn and Errol looked at each other and smiled. They'd already viewed the terrace that from the many windows of the living room. Shrugging, they followed him.

"It's a bit of the country right here in the heart of the city," the agent said as he opened the door and mounted the steps that brought them to the rooftop garden.

"This is spectacular," Tar gushed.

"You have a spa, sauna and gym.

"I'm already looking forward to making love to you up here," Errol whispered in her ear.

She giggled and shot a sidelong glance at the agent who appeared not to have heard him.

"That settles it then. Let's close this deal. I can have my things moved here before you can say *paté de foie gras*."

The real estate agent discreetly left them alone to discuss the matter all the same.

"Don't be too impulsive, Errol."

Setting his fists on his hips, he turned to her. "Why are you doing this, Tar?"

"Doing what?"

"I don't know. You're impeding our progress? You're holding us back. I thought you wanted this. It doesn't get much better than this, Tar." He took both of her hands in his. "I thought you wanted to be with me. I thought you wanted to marry me. Are you having second thoughts?"

"No. I do want to marry you, Errol. I want all this, but it just isn't the right time. Please try to understand."

He pressed his lips together. "Okay. Fine."

She glanced at her watch. That morning, she'd quickly check the flights out of Paris on the internet and there was one leaving in just under an hour. "Look, it's too late for me to catch a flight today, so I'll stay another day, but tomorrow…"

He smiled. "And you can bet I'll take advantage of every minute of this last night together.

"But seriously, Errol, first thing tomorrow…"

"Not first thing. I have an early class tomorrow morning." He pulled her into his arms. "I can take you to the airport afterward... at two o'clock."

"I can take a cab, Errol. You don't have to..."

He huffed his frustration. "I want to take my fiancé to the airport, Tar. No disrespect to your mother, but I'm sure she can handle another few hours with my crew."

She had no reasonable argument for that. "Okay, I'll stay a few hours more." Getting on her tiptoes, she reached up to kiss him. "As much as I hate to go, tomorrow I will leave."

He kissed her back, pulled her tightly to him and groaned his displeasure. "I'll go wrap things up with the real estate agent, and we'll head to the hotel after that. I want to start ravaging you as soon as possible."

Taryn followed him inside and remained in the kitchen while he headed to the agent in the living room. She watched him walk away feeling suddenly guilty for making him go through all this while she returned to New York. It didn't make sense that he should sell his apartment and move just because she's afraid of the dark. Then again, it showed his commitment, didn't it?

"Let's go," he said when he returned a few moments later. "Everything is settled."

In the car on the way to the hotel, Taryn felt she had to say something, but the words wouldn't come. Only when they reached their luxurious and spacious room did she finally speak her mind.

"Errol, I feel awful about this. It's unreasonable for you to move because of me while I return to New York."

"I anticipate you'll come back, won't you?"

"Yes, of course, but…"

"Then it's settled. There's no point putting it off. By the time you get back, I'll be in the new place and you'll have nothing to fear."

Taryn sat back on the king sized bed. "It's just that I know how you already have so much to take care of… what with your restaurant in New York burning down and everything. It's selfish of me to add this to your problems."

He sat beside her and ran his hand from the curve of her neck down between her breasts. "I don't want to spend the last moments I have with you discussing all this. I want to taste you, and savor you, and fill my soul up with you."

Cupping her breast, he laid her back and covered her lips with his own. His hands trembled as he pulled her shirt up, exposing her breasts to his ravenous mouth.

"I can't get enough of the taste of your skin."

"I want your skin, too," Tar said as she reached for the zipper of his pants. If she had to leave him again for a few weeks, she wanted to leave him with something to remember. She wanted to drive him crazy, make him so horny he'd remember this night forever.

She pulled out his already hardened shaft, brought it to her mouth for one single long suck then slid his erection between her breasts. Pushing her breasts together to better squeeze his erection, she glided her voluminous orbs over the length of him.

"You wild siren, damn I love you." He grabbed her wrists, jerked her further up on the bed and straddled her. "I want to fuck you. I want to screw you. I want to make love to you. I want you, Tar. I want you."

He jacked her skirt up and pushed his erection deep inside her, filling her with his arousal, filling her with his love, filling her with memories that would cling to her for weeks on end.

Wrapping her arms around him, she held him close, kissed his chest, his neck, and his cheek before finally finding his lips. She never wanted to let him go.

And hours later, when he took her for the third time, she seriously questioned her decision to return to New York. They were so good together, it was impossible to imagine being away from him again. How would she survive another few weeks without his touch? How would she manage to concentrate on her responsibilities back home when all she wanted was to touch him again?

# Chapter 10

While Errol prepared to go to his morning class, Taryn contemplated him from the luxurious sheets of the large bed. The hotel room was spectacular, rich and elegant, and she couldn't help but wonder how he could afford such a luxury while his restaurant lay in ruins.

"How are things going with La Benicoise?" she asked without thinking. She'd managed to keep from mentioning the burnt down eatery all weekend, but her curiosity finally won over.

He shrugged as he buttoned up his crisp white shirt. "Not so great. The insurance company isn't satisfied with the reports they've received. I'm thinking it might just be easier to sell."

Stunned, she looked at him wide-eyed. "Selling? Isn't that a little bit drastic. I mean, this is your baby."

"It's quickly turning into a headache. I just don't know if it's worth it anymore. Besides, it's not like I don't have plenty to occupy my time with."

"I couldn't ever imagine giving up Sam's so easily."

He pulled the zipper of his slacks up and shot her a questioning glare. "I'm not giving it up so easily, Tar."

Taryn couldn't help but notice how defensive he sounded. Suddenly, Matt's words came back to her. It was inconceivable; Errol would never torch his own restaurant. Then again, never would she have thought she'd hear him say he wanted to sell the place.

On the other hand, if he sold the restaurant, he would no longer have to have contact with Suzanne. That alone would be well worth watching him sell his New York eatery.

Pulling on his jacket he looked at her with hungry eyes.

"Are you sure you won't change your mind… about leaving? I could be back here at two and fuck you the rest of the day."

"I'm sure, Errol." She chuckled and patted his clean shaven cheek. "Though the thought of us naked and making love all afternoon sure sounds tempting."

"You know, you leave me no choice but to go back to New York the minute I have enough episodes in the can. While I'm there I can take a closer look at what's going on at La Benicoise."

Taryn smiled, but in the back of her mind, all she wanted to do was talk to him about Matt's suspicions, but felt it wouldn't go over very well. Instead, she changed the subject altogether.

"Last night I was thinking of your offer to sell your apartment to buy the one we visited yesterday."

"Isn't it a great apartment?"

"It is, but don't you think it's a bit much. I mean, what if you can't sell yours?"

He smiled and grabbed a quick sip of coffee. "I know someone who's been dying to get his hands on that apartment. For the past three years he's asked if I'm ready to sell… something about setting up a nice little nest for his honey. Apparently, it has everything he wants and needs; close enough to his work place to make nightly calls easily, but far away enough from his wife to keep the relationship discreet."

Shocked, Taryn gaped at him. "That's horrible."

Chuckling, Errol cupped her chin and tilted her head up for a quick, but loving kiss. "Indeed it is horrible, but if he wants my apartment, I'll sell it to him. All I have to do is make one phone call and the deal is done."

"But, Errol, that's what I wanted to talk to you about. Don't you think it's too drastic?"

"We've already been through this, Taryn." He turned to look at her, his eyes suddenly dark. "Unless you're telling me you don't want to come back to Paris."

"Of course, I'm going to come back."

"Do you want to marry me, Taryn?"

"What a silly question. Of course I do."

Pensive, he nodded and grabbed his briefcase. "I've got to go," he finally said as he slipped into his shoes and grabbed his keys. "Order breakfast, have a relaxing morning and I'll be back in a few hours to bring you to the airport." He tenderly kissed her lips before leaving.

Alone in the hotel room, Taryn spun Matt's words around and around in her head. Getting the insurance money would probably solve a lot of Errol's problems, more so than if he'd simply tried to sell the restaurant.

Then she considered his offer to sell his apartment. Everything was going so fast and she was beginning to feel rushed and exhausted by the overflow of emotions

After her third coffee and a few bites of her toast, she decided to take a cab down to the Institute. Getting to the airport would be a lot quicker if they didn't have to return to the hotel. Besides, she missed how the Institute touched all her senses, bringing her alive with all the sights and smells of fine cuisine. She wanted to take a little peek before leaving.

She gathered her few belongings and headed down to the lobby where the clerk called her a cab. Within fifteen minutes she was at the Institute and after dropping off her luggage in Errol's office, she headed to his class to surprise him.

The class of about fifteen students had only one male. The others were all young females who looked at Errol like a god. Pretty, bright-eyed, eager and sprite, they all had the same look in their eyes. That look of adoration, of hunger, of curiosity.

A sudden pang of insecure jealousy strangled Tar as she stood watching Errol smile at the young students. His eyes sparkled and his smile was warm. He was all sex and charm… and completely approachable; too approachable.

Taryn scanned the room of pretty girls. A few were too obvious, making the conquest for Errol too easy and therefore unattractive to him. Others were eager to seduce him, but the look in their eyes bordered on desperation. She knew Errol would never want a desperate woman. But a few of them, barely a handful, were as pure, innocent and naively enamored with him as she had been.

How long would it take Errol to forget her and choose a new conquest? How long before he grew hungry for female companionship and succumbed to one of his beautiful, young students? How long before he tired of this game of flying from New York to Paris and back to New York again?

Probably not very long. After all, if he could have a pretty girl on his arm at all times, right here in Paris, why bother with the trouble of a girl who is all the way over in New York.

The thought made her physically ill and she leaned against the wall for support. She loved him, with all her heart, but her insecurities were quickly taking over.

Maybe it was too good to be true; believing that he could possibly settle down and marry a girl like her. Men like him didn't marry girls like her. They rarely married at all. And if they did, they went on to have numerous mistresses, some as early as the very first weeks of marriage.

She suddenly thought of the friend who wanted to buy his apartment. Could Errol, one day, find an apartment in which he'd regularly go find his lover?

His class was almost over. Taryn's heart wanted to reach out to Errol, to talk to him about her doubts. She wanted him to reassure her, to tell her that he loved her… and only her.

But her pride also told her to hold her head up high and be strong. She couldn't possibly spend all her time questioning and doubting him. What kind of relationship would that be?

Just as the pretty girls and the lone guy left the large room and Taryn was about to enter, a tall and beautiful woman entered by the rear door; Madame X. Oozing confidence and sex appeal, she sauntered up to Errol, her brow cocked in arousal and the promise of a seduction.

Wearing a dark blue, come fuck me dress and sky high black stilettos, she was everything but unthreatening. She kissed Errol's cheeks, put her hands atop his shoulders and patted his arms in a show of appreciation for his toned muscles.

Taryn felt the blood quickly rise to her cheeks at the sight, but making matters worse was the look in Errol's eyes. He was pleased to see this temptress this vixen who dared touch him. His eyes welcomed her, lured her, charmed her. They dipped voluntarily into the wild woman's deep, deep cleavage.

Damn it, Taryn fumed. She'd hadn't even left Paris yet and he was ogling another woman. Not only that, but he allowed this other woman to put her hands all over him.

Absent-mindedly, Taryn played with the ring on her finger. She'd been stupid to accept his proposal to begin with. She'd been stupid to believe he could ever want to marry her at all.

Maybe she should just call the whole thing off before she really got hurt, before she became fully invested.

Before she exploded right there in front of them and made a fool of herself, she silently turned down the hall and walked out of the Institute. She picked up her luggage in Errol's apartment and hailed a cab.

It was a horrible way to end such a fantastic weekend, but it was time she woke up and smelled the coffee. Errol wasn't the kind of man to settle down, and he never would; not with her; not with anyone else.

# Chapter 11

Tar walked blindly through the airport paying little attention to the people around her. As usual the airport was busy as vacationers, business people and visitors ran around looking for their terminal. She could hear the distant chatter as people left family members and loved ones at various terminals. Disheartened, she winced at the warm words of departure that surrounded her: *au revoir, à la prochaine, bon voyage*. It all made her hasty departure from Paris all the more painful.

"Taryn?"

Though she heard the excited call of her name in some closed off corner of her consciousness, she paid no attention and walked on. The only person who knew her was Errol and she wanted nothing to do with him.

"Tar. Hey, Taryn." A handsome young man jumped in front of her. "Taryn, where are you heading?"

Deeply entrenched in her heartache and anger for Errol, she barely focused on the young man in front of her. At first bleary glance, she didn't recognize him and was a little irritated by his pursuit of her.

"Tar, it's me… Henri." He flashed her a brilliant smile and put a friendly hand to her shoulder.

"Henri," she finally managed as she brought her steady gaze to his beaming face. "Oh, Henri. I'm sorry. I'm so lost in thought, I can barely see straight."

"I can see that. I've been following you and calling your name since you turned the corner. You seemed awfully deep in thought... and not too happy about it either. Is everything all right?"

"Everything is fine, Henri. And what are you doing here? Where are you off to?"

Henri checked his watch. "You know what? I have about half an hour before my flight. How 'bout you?"

I have forever, she wanted to say. Angry with Errol, she'd not even thought of the time and had made her way to the airport a full two hours ahead of her scheduled flight.

"How about a good cup of coffee before you board?" he offered when she didn't answer.

She nodded. "That'd be great. I think I have quite a long wait ahead of me."

"Great. Come on. I know this great little place that serves decent coffee and some great pastries."

At the coffee shop, Henri ordered while Tar sat at a nearby table. She tried to muster up a happy mood to hide how she truly felt. If she kept her glum expression, he'd surely question her about it and talking about Errol, especially with Henri, was the last thing she wanted to do.

"*Merci*," she said as he arrived with two steaming cups of coffee and two *mille feuilles*.

"My pleasure."

She took a sip of hot coffee. "So where are you off to?"

"Switzerland."

"You going to visit your family?"

"Yeah. Duty calls. I'll be visiting one of our family farms there."

"Duty?"

He chuckled. "My father tried to get out of his tractor too fast when he thought he'd run over the dog. He hopped off that big tractor tire and twisted his ankle. My mother called and asked me to come lend a hand for a few days."

"That's so sweet of you, Henri."

"Timing is perfect. I'm up to date with all of my assignments, and I had this incredible craving for my mom's *boeuf bourgignon*." He drummed his fingers along the edge of his coffee cup. "You left so fast the other time… and then you just cut classes without saying anything to anyone."

Tar chuckled. "I don't think anyone else in the class really cared one way or the other. You know, you're the only friend I have from the Institute."

"Well then, as your only friend from the Institute, can I ask how you've been?"

"Great. Just great."

"That's a pretty lackluster 'great'. Your sudden absence from class was explained with a family emergency back home. Is that why you didn't even say goodbye?"

She didn't want to lie to him, but she couldn't very well tell him the truth about her falling out with Errol. She nodded. "My mother had a nasty fall and hurt her hip pretty bad. She's just now getting back on her feet." While it wasn't the reason she'd returned to New York, it wasn't a bald faced lie either.

"Funny… I go to Switzerland to help my father and you went to the United States to help you mother."

She smiled and shrugged. "I guess for all the time they've tended to our scraped knees and cut fingers, it's the least we can do."

He bit into his *mille feuilles* and looked thoughtfully at her. "How are things with Errol?"

Startled, Tar clumsily set her coffee cup down then tried to casually pick up her pastry.

"I kind of couldn't help but figure there was something going on between you two. I mean, the way he just busted his way in at my place and… well, he pretty much made it clear that you belong to him… well, you know, that you're his girl… you know what I mean."

Tar smiled as Henri fumbled for the right words to describe her relationship with Errol.

"I mean, I can understand he would want to keep you all to himself. If you were my girl, I would…" He looked sheepishly at her. "Anyway... and now, what brings you back to Paris? I didn't see you at the Institute."

"I had a few things to settle."

"And now you're going off to...?"

"Back to New York. I hadn't really planned to stay in Paris more than a few days." At least she didn't have to lie about that.

"You know I really missed you in class. It wasn't the same without you. All the other students are so stuck up and pretentious, and all the girls, well... It's just not the same."

"You're sweet, Henri. I appreciate that. And believe me, I've missed you too. I really hate that I had to leave the Institute before finishing my classes."

"Any plans to come back to finish what you started?"

"I'll see. Maybe I'll have a few classes with you when I start again."

He shook his head. "Actually, I've already finished."

Her eyes popped open. "How? I still have almost a year to go before I finish."

"Like I said... when you left things weren't the same. I just decided I didn't want to waste any time, so I took a few extra classes and now... well, I'm pretty much ready to go out into the world and wow them with my culinary knowledge."

"And I'm sure that's exactly what you're going to do. I have no doubt."

"But just because I'm not going to the Institute anymore doesn't mean I wouldn't be thrilled to see you if ever you return to Paris." He let the offer hang in the air an uncomfortable moment. "So what did you have to settle in a matter of a few days?"

Tar didn't miss a beat. "I left so quickly the last time, I left a few things at the Institute and I had a few documents I needed signed." She took a sip of coffee and looked thoughtfully at her one French friend. "Can I ask you something?"

"Sure. Go ahead."

"How…" She stopped herself, embarrassed by the question she so longed to hear the answer to. "When I left… the last time…"

Henri cocked his head to the side and furrowed his brow.

"Well, I was just wondering how… people reacted."

"You know how people are. They're so caught up in their studies and assignments and everything… not many people noticed, to tell you the truth."

Taryn chuckled uncomfortably and cleared her throat. "Well, actually, I was thinking of one particular person."

"Oh," Henri exclaimed with a burst of laughter. "How silly of me. Of course… Errol. You want to know how Errol…"

"Yes. Yes," she said eagerly.

He pressed his lips together and nearly drove Tar nuts.

"So?"

"At first I didn't really get it. It was subtle. You know how Errol can be; strict, harsh, uncompromising. Well, all that intensified. He was sour and bitter and inexplicably cruel. A few days after you left we had to make bouillabaisse. You should have heard the comments he made. One girl's dish smelled like a sewer. Another one looked like baby spit. And, well, I don't think I need to tell you how he was with me. From that moment on, nothing I did was right. My creams were too runny. My meringue was too stiff. My steaks were too seared and my vegetables too soggy."

"I'm sorry about that. I hate to think that all this had an adverse effect on you. He shouldn't have done that."

He shrugged. "Don't worry. It was all talk. For all of his barking and shouting, in the end he gave me fair grades."

"Good." She'd hoped he'd give her a little more details about Errol's behavior with regards to her departure, not his grades.

Henri reached out and covered her hand with his. "It took me a few days, but I realized he was heartbroken. All of his lashing out was simply his clumsy way of dealing with it. I mean, I don't think anyone else picked up on what was really going on. The only reason I suspected it was the scene I'd witnessed when he came to get you at my place."

A ray of hope filled her. "You think he was really heartbroken?"

"Definitely."

She didn't want to be so obviously happy, to smile so broadly, but she couldn't help it. The weight that had had her dragging her feet since seeing Errol in class with Madame X was finally lifted.

For all his faults, Errol did love her.

Henri squeezed her hand, pressing her engagement ring into her flesh. He quickly released her hand and looked at the bejeweled finger. His brow rose, furrowed and rose again.

"Uh… is that…? Are you… with him?"

She heard the pain and loss in his awkward question.

"I mean, I know Monsieur King is known for, well… but…" He picked up her finger and stared at the brilliant diamond. "He is not known for this."

"I'll admit I was a little surprised, too."

"So it's really serious between you two. I mean, I thought it was just…"

"A fling?"

He shrugged. "He doesn't exactly have a reputation for monog…"

Right, she thought.

"But a tiger can change his stripes," he quickly added.

*Yeah, right.* Her sudden high was quickly deflated.

"I do hope he'll treat you right."

She was tempted to tell him how he'd already failed at that. She desperately needed to share with someone what she'd recently witnessed.

"I'm sure he will," he went on. "But if he ever slips back to his old ways, well, you know you can always talk to me."

Did he suspect she already had so much she wanted to say to him? As a French man, perhaps Henri could give her insight into Errol's ways. Could he shed light on the questions she had about her relationship with him?

She didn't want to risk it… not yet.

"If you need me for anything, Taryn…" He squeezed her hand. "All you have to do is call."

Hesitating a long time, Tar stared at the remainder of her *mille feuilles*. She'd barely touched the pastry. Though her stomach rumbled with hunger, she just didn't have the appetite for the perfectly flaky dessert.

"You know," she finally said. "There is something you could do."

"Anything. Just name it."

"Could you keep an eye on Errol for me?"

He grimaced a quick second then pressed a smile. "I guess."

"I know you're not at the Institute much anymore, but… well, just keep an eye and ear open."

With a smile that didn't quite hide his disappointment, he checked his watch and stood. "The minute I get back, I'll be all over him."

Tar got to her feet and reached out to hug him. "You're such a great friend, Henri. You really are."

He hugged her back, but there was nothing friendly about it. Pressing her body to his, he silently let her know just how he felt about her.

"Have a nice visit with your family," Tar said as she pulled back. She kissed his cheeks, quick friendly pecks meant to cool the heat she felt radiating from him.

The quick pecks didn't have the expected reaction. Henri pulled her into his arms and kissed her lips.

"Henri," she whispered as she pulled back.

He held her and brought his lips over hers once more. His kiss was tender and full of yearning. "Just a kiss for good luck." His eyes met hers with a world full of promises and a heart filled with love.

She put her hand to his cheek and smiled. Life would be so much simpler if she could love a man like him. He had all the qualities any girl would die for. Good looking, strong, smart, caring, always ready to make her laugh.

"I'd better go," Henri muttered.

"Yes," she whispered.

She watched him walk away then finally turned to head to the terminal that would have her home in a few hours.

# Chapter 12

Taryn spent an endless hour in the terminal flipping through a magazine she'd bought, though she realized it was a complete waste of money. She simply stared blankly at one page after another, until she came to a true or false love quiz. *25 Questions You Need to Ask Yourself Before You Say I do.*

"Seriously?" she muttered to herself. The timing couldn't be more dreadful. She looked at the furrowed brow of the model who stood looking at her diamond engagement ring amidst a bedroom strewn with dirty socks, underwear, a few ties and mixed matched shoes. Her other hand had a death grip on a crisp, white man's shirt… with lipstick on the collar.

This should be fun, she thought wryly.

*His lifestyle is in tune with mine.*

Hmm, she mused. "We both enjoy cooking so." True.

*His love makes me feel secure.*

"Well, sort of."

*We both see a bright future for our love.*

"I thought I did."

*When I'm away, I know I can trust him.*

Tar slammed the magazine shut and tossed it on the seat beside her. “Stupid quiz.”

Her phone rang, startling her. She checked the number and realized it was Errol. “Speak of the devil,” she muttered. It rang a second and third time while she simply stared at the phone. Was she ready to talk to him?

A fourth ring.

He’ll just sweet talk his way out of it, she thought.

Fifth ring.

But I want to hear what he’ll say.

Just as she pressed the button to take the call, it stopped ringing.

It’s just as well.

Moments later her phone signaled the arrival of a text.

*Honey, where are you?*

Playing innocent, she thought. It was just like him.

Fired up, she fired off a brief reply.

*At the airport.*

Her phone rang again, and once more she let it ring, uncertain she wanted to hear his voice. But on the fourth ring, she picked up.

“Tar?”

“Were you expecting someone else?” she quipped.

“Tar where are you?”

“Didn’t you get my text? I’m at the airport.”

“Yes, I got your text, but I didn’t understand.”

"What's not to understand? I have to get back to New York and the airport is the best way to go."

"Tar, what's going on? I hurried home and found the apartment empty. I thought maybe you'd come back to the Institute to find me, but you weren't there either. Did something happen back home to make you rush off?"

"No… nothing back home. Something here at home."

"What does that mean?"

"Errol, I love you, but…"

"But…? But what? Tar, what the hell is going on?"

"Don't get angry with me, Errol King. You have no right being upset with me."

"I'm not upset with you, Tar. I was worried. I've been running around looking for you for almost an hour. You didn't even leave a note."

"Maybe you should ask Madame X if she has a note."

"What?"

"Your friend, Madame X. Why don't you just go back and chat with her?"

"Tar, what are you talking about?"

"You know, I just read a quiz that says we're not compatible."

"Now you're just talking silly."

Grinding her teeth, she realized he had a point, but she couldn't stop herself from going on. She was on a roll… an angry roll. “Look, Errol, I just don’t think I can be with a man like you. I mean, maybe a more worldly woman could stay with a womanizing man like yourself, but I can’t. I want a man who’ll only have eyes for me. Do you understand that?”

“Tar, we’ve talked about this. I may have known a few women in the past, but now… you know you’re the only one for me. You're accusing me of something I didn’t do.”

“Liar! I saw you, Errol. I was there and I saw you.”

“Saw what? Where?”

“At the Institute. You and Madame X. As flirtatious as usual, she was all over you and you enjoyed it.”

“You were at the Institute? Why didn’t you come see me?”

“I was going to, but you were so busy with Madame X, I didn’t want to interrupt.”

“Tar, you're overreacting. It’s not what you think.”

“Are you going to deny you enjoyed it? Cause it was written all over your face, Errol. You were beaming… beaming like when we first met, when you wanted to have me.”

“Tar, stop this nonsense.”

“That’s exactly what I intend to do, Errol. I’m putting an end to all this nonsense. And it’s about time.” Before he could say another word, she hung up. As she prepared to toss her phone into her purse, it rang again. This time, she closed her purse and let it ring.

"*Le vol 533 presentement a l'guirit 6.* Flight 533 now boarding at Gate 6."

It's about time, she wanted to complain. She grabbed her carry on and hurried to board the plane. Eager to put as much distance as possible between herself and Errol, she stomped onto the plane and threw herself into her seat. The woman already settled in the window seat glared at her, but Tar didn't care. She was in no mood to be polite and nice.

Seconds later, guilt got the best of her and she turned to the woman and smiled. Before she could apologize, her phone rang, startling her. Shooting a sheepish glance at the woman, she tried to ignore her phone.

"You may as well answer. You'll have to turn it off in a few minutes."

"I know who the caller is and I'm not really in the mood to talk to him." Never the type to share her personal life, she couldn't believe she'd just made such a statement to a complete stranger.

"Don't tell me you hooked up with one of those irresistible French men."

Tar simply pressed her lips together and tried to put up a brave front, but her lashes quickly lined with tears and she cast her gaze to her feet.

The woman rummaged through her purse. "I think I have a tissue in here somewhere."

"I'm all right," Tar muttered.

"Right."

A tissue appeared in front of Tar's face, but it wasn't the feminine hand of the woman beside her who held it. It was a strong and familiar masculine hand.

Tar looked up. "Errol," she whispered as she met his warm gaze. "What are you… How did you…? This is… but… You can't…"

"Had you stuck around a moment longer, you would have seen me push Madame X away. You would have also heard me tell her that I was taken."

Stunned, Tar stared at him while her heart turned multiple somersaults.

"I made it clear that I was in love with a very special woman who satisfied me in every conceivable way."

Tar shook her head clear and took the tissue he offered. Unable to rip her disbelieving gaze from his face, she wiped her tears.

"Had you stayed a moment longer, you wouldn't be wiping those tears." He reached for her hand. "I'm going to have to do something to calm that jealous streak of yours."

"You both seemed so… cozy."

"I was seething as I tried to remain calm and polite before her aggressive come on. I do have a professional reputation to think of. I can't just blow up in class. I quietly and calmly let her know how I felt."

"I'm sorry, Errol, I just…"

Errol cocked a brow at the woman in the window seat. Her eyes wide with envy and admiration, she stared at Errol a moment longer before tapping Tar's knee.

"I'll leave you a private moment."

Tar scooted over and Errol sat beside her, his arm quickly snaking around her.

"When I realized you'd run off without saying a word…I couldn't believe it. Tar, don't you realize how much I love you? I wouldn't do anything to jeopardize what I have with you." He leaned in to kiss her, but his warm kiss was interrupted by the flight attendant.

"I'll have to ask you to put away your carry-on and fasten your seatbelts."

"Gladly," Errol said with a beaming grin. He stood and tossed his carry-on into the overhead compartment and sat down again, nudging even closer to Taryn.

"What exactly do you think you're doing, Errol? The plane is going to take off any minute now. If you don't stop this nonsense and get off the plane, you'll end up in New York."

"And where are you going, Tar?"

"To New York," she spat.

"Well, then, that's where I'm going."

"Errol, you can't."

"Not only can I, but apparently I must."

"Why?"

"Because you won't listen to reason."

Playing with the ring on her finger, Tar stared blindly at the back of the seat in front of her. "You know, Errol, even if what you say is true about your reaction to Madame X, we both know that this can't work."

"I know nothing of the sort."

"You're not the marrying kind, Errol. You never have been and you never will be. I think we should both face that fact before we get hurt… or rather before I get hurt."

"You don't think this hurts me? Having you run off like this? Without saying a word, without giving me a chance to defend myself, explain myself."

With everyone seated and belted in, one of the flight attendants gave the passengers all the safety directives. Taryn barely heard her. Her ears were too tuned in to every word Errol spoke.

"We're taking off," she murmured as the plane taxied down the runway.

"I'm aware of that."

"You're wasting your time, Errol. You have so much to take care of here and you're wasting your time flying all the way to New York. You'll only have to fly back, you know."

The plane picked up speed as did Taryn's heart rate.

Errol reached for her hand and held it in a warm embrace.

Taryn glanced out the window just as the plane's wheels left the ground. They rose into the air, leaving them with a last glimpse of the Parisian skyline. Soon they pierced the clouds and the dull grey day was left below them while the afternoon sun seared through the tiny window.

"Beautiful, isn't it?" Errol whispered into her ear.

While she nodded, she was eager to receive her mid-flight drink. The flight attendant was slowly rolling her cart down the aisle handing out drinks and snacks to all the passengers who needed the diversion.

"White wine," Errol firmly said the moment the flight attendant arrived.

Efficient and cordial, he twisted off the cap of a miniature bottle of wine, poured it into two miniature wine glasses and handed them to Errol.

"Here," Errol said as he handed her a glass. "Stop fidgeting and have a sip."

"I'm not fidgeting," she argued as she took the glass and enjoyed a sip.

He smiled and set a calm hand on her bobbing knee. "Really."

She huffed. "So I'm a bit jittery, that's all. You have me turned upside down, not knowing what I should think or feel."

"You're beautiful when you're angry," he said.

"Don't change the subject. You play with my feelings, Errol. You're toying with my emotions, and I can't deal with it. I'm not the type of woman who can handle a man like you. I wish I were. I wish I could.

Maybe I'm just not strong enough. I'm not one of those strong-willed, secure women who can just watch her man ogle every passing woman and flirt with co-workers and…" She let out a long, exasperated breath. "I'm just not that woman, Errol."

*****

# Errol

Errol sat back, smiled and quietly sipped his wine. He knew she was a lot stronger than she let on, than she realized herself, but he no longer knew what he could say to make her see just how much he loved her. Time, he thought. What she needed was time alone with him, time to see just how much he wanted and needed her… just how much he treasured her.

For the time being, he let her take in what he'd already said. Surely his very presence on the plane was proof of his love. Were she any of the flaky women he'd known in his life, he'd be at home completely unaffected by her departure.

An hour later, meals were brought to them.

"It's not every day we have a world renowned chef on board," the flight attendant said, all too aware of the quality of food he was about to serve. "We do make every attempt to serve the highest quality food."

"I'm sure you do."

"Beef or chicken?" The simple offering brought a tint of red to the man's face.

"I'll have the chicken and she'll have the beef."

Taryn glared at Errol, but said nothing until the flight attendant wheeled his way onto the next row.

"What makes you think I want beef? I wanted the chicken."

"I know," he said as he lowered her table from the back of the seat in front of her. "That's why I asked for one of each."

Feeling like a sleepy child who only wanted to complain about anything and everything, she glared at him. "You didn't know. If you'd known you would have told him the chicken was for me."

"All right. I knew that whatever I ordered you wouldn't want it."

"Are you accusing me of deliberately contradicting you?"

"Are you denying it?"

She clucked her tongue and narrowed her eyes. "You're not winning any points with all this, you know."

They ate in virtual silence and even bit back on comments regarding the food. While the airline may make every attempt to serve high quality food, the flavor was sorely lacking.

After their trays were cleared away, Tar tilted her seat back as far as she could without lying on the lap of the man behind her. Without a word, she closed her eyes and feigned sleep.

Though far from satisfied with his meal, Errol's belly was nonetheless full. A few brief moments of shut-eye wouldn't hurt. After all, he'd been keeping hellish hours lately and a little nap would do him good.

It didn't take long for him to nod off. The gentle rumbling of the plane rocked him and the strong purr of the motors lulled him. He felt Taryn's soft and warm body beside him and gladly allowed the sensations to fill his dreams.

He was already breathless as he swept her up in his arms, pulled her onto an endless bed and ripped her clothes off, revealing her exquisite luscious body. She was hot and sweating, excited by his animal ways.

She fought him, scrambling to get off the bed, but he held her tight and cooed gentle words into her ear. She struggled harder and her breaths now came in short, sharp pants. At first he thought it was the excitement of their encounter, but he soon realized her breaths were filled with fear and anxiety.

Her short, sharp pants were soon replaced with quiet whimpers.

Errol struggled to wakefulness as the sounds he heard no longer made sense. He knew the scene she'd witnessed between himself and Madame X had hurt her, but the cries he heard were not those of heartache, but of something else.

She's frightened, he thought.

Her shaking finally brought him to full wakefulness. He opened his eyes and was surprised by the intense darkness that surrounded them. For a moment he thought he was still asleep, still caught up in a dream, but he realized all the lights were out and the sun had long left them.

Now fully awake and alert, he leaned closer to Tar and realized she was not only shaking, she was shuddering.

"Tar, don't worry. I'm here."

She muttered something unintelligible and continued to shake more and more violently.

"I want to get out," she suddenly blurted out as she pushed him off her.

"Tar, we're on a plane. Wake up."

"I want to get out of here. Errol, get me out."

"Taryn, we should be landing soon," he said, though he had no idea how much further they had to travel.

"I don't care." She stood and tried to kick her way past him. "I want to get out. I want to get out!"

He took a firm hold of her arm and pulled her back into her seat, quickly buckling her in. Wrapping his arms around her, he finally realized what was going on.

The same irrational fear of the dark that had so terrified her on that dreaded night in Paris. He'd heard of people who were afraid of the dark before, but had never seen someone become so petrified.

She cowered in her seat, rolled up into a fetal position while strange sounds came from her mouth. Every once in a while, he legs jerked awkwardly, as if in a frightened spasm.

Errol pulled her closer to him. "Tar, close your eyes. Just close your eyes and concentrate on my arms around you." He tried to lean in closer to kiss her, but she turned away. Unrelenting, he tried again, this time taking a firm hold of her cheeks and turning her to him. He pressed his lips over hers. She fought back a moment, but finally softened in his arms as he slowly and reassuringly slipped his tongue into her mouth.

"I'm here, Tar," he whispered between hot kisses. "I'm not going to let anything happen to you."

"Don't leave me, Errol," she murmured as her fingers dug into his arms.

"I'm staying right here until we get off this plane together."

"Don't leave."

He kissed her again, putting as much warmth and reassurance into each kiss as he could.

"Never," he whispered. "I'm never leaving."

# Chapter 13

The lights flickered, but refused to remain on for another ten minutes. When they finally stayed on, Errol glanced at Tar sleeping in his arms. It was hard to believe she could now be so calm in sleep considering how violently she'd trembled once darkness fell upon them. He brushed her hair off her face and kissed her temples, not wishing to wake her, while longing to sooth and reassure her.

Her lips moved in silent murmurings as she remained deep in sleep.

"Is everything all right here?" the flight attendant asked as he passed through the aisle reassuring passengers.

"Yes," Errol said. "We're fine, but could you bring her a ginger ale and an aspirin. I have a feeling she's going to have a nasty headache when she wakes up."

The flight attendant rummaged through his cart and gave Errol a can of soda and a little plastic bag with two aspirins.

Tar stirred as Errol thanked the young man.

"The lights are back on," she grumbled, squinting in the harsh light.

"Yeah. How are you feeling?"

She sat up and patted her cheek, opening and closing her mouth wide. "It feels like someone punched me in the jaw."

"It wasn't me," Errol said with a chuckle. "I think you may have grinded your teeth a little too much."

"I guess."

"I got you a soda and a few aspirins."

"You'd think I had a hangover."

"At least with a hangover, you have the consolation of having a good time the night before. I don't think you really had a good time when the lights went out."

She reached for the soda and aspirins. "You have a point."

"I've never seen you so scared."

"Have you forgotten that time at your place?" She popped the aspirins into her mouth and cracked open the can of pop for a few sips.

"No, but I have to say this time was even worse. I didn't think I'd ever succeed in calming you down."

She looked into his eyes. "But you did. I don't know how, but you did."

"Good thing considering the lights were out for almost an hour."

"I'm sorry I freaked out like that."

He was silent a long moment as he contemplated his next question. "Are you really that afraid of the dark?"

Tar shrugged and looked out the window. "It's nothing that out of the ordinary. A lot of people don't like the dark."

"I agree, but few people become hysterical in the dark."

She turned to glare at him. "All right, so I'm nyctophobic."

"That's nothing to be ashamed of, Tar. We all have our fears."

"I'm not ashamed, it's just not a topic I enjoy discussing."

"Maybe talking about it a bit can help."

"I don't really know what I can tell you. I've always been afraid of the dark. I mean darkened streets at night or a dark room won't really scare me, but total darkness, pitch black… I don't know why, but it makes me feel trapped, like the walls are closing in on me. For a long time when I was a little girl I'd have this recurring nightmare. I was always being chased by I don't know what. I'd run behind bushes when I was outside, but sometimes I was chased inside and I'd hide in the closet or in an armoire. But that armoire would always turn into a prison, trapping me inside and keeping me in total darkness, and I can't get out."

Errol took a hold of her hand and held it tight, trying his best to transmit his understanding.

"The nightmares were so real, it was incredible. The first few times I'd had them, I'd wake up to a dark room; a dark house. It was as if the nightmare continued on even while I was awake. I didn't really want to tell my mother. I mean, at nine years old I was supposed to be a big girl and the idea of asking for a nightlight was so embarrassing."

"So what d'you do?"

She smiled for the first time since waking. "I got a small allowance for helping out around the house. I saved it up and finally bought a nightlight. I was in such a rush to buy it that I couldn't wait until I'd raised enough money to buy it in a retail store. I found one in a thrift shop for a buck and a half. I was thrilled."

"Did you ever tell your mother?"

Chuckling, she pried his fingers off her hand and toyed with them. "No, but I think she knew. I mean, she'd get up in the middle of the night to go to the bathroom or something, so surely she saw the light coming from my room, but she never said anything."

"But they were just nightmares. Why are you still so affected by them?"

She shrugged. "I don't know. The sensations I feel while trapped in that darkened nightmare stay with me long after I wake up; this feeling of being enclosed and unable to get out, of being hungry and thirsty and cold; the feeling that I'll never be found and never able to get out. When I was in middle school, a boy brought me to the closet in his room to kiss me. He never had a chance. The moment he closed the door I just freaked."

Errol pulled her into his arms. "My poor baby. I hate to see you so out of sorts." He wanted to ask more questions, but she'd already begun to tremble. "Don't go back to that dark place," he coaxed, trying to bring her out of the black nightmare that haunted her so much. He never would have thought simply talking about it would make her tremble again. As he held her in his arms, he knew that whatever he could do to help her get over it, he would. She was the most precious person in his life, and it surprised him how much he ached to see her so frightened like that. All he wanted to do was to hold her tight and make sure she would be safe.

# Chapter 14

## Errol

While part of him regretted questioning her at all, another part of him wanted to know more about this uncontrollable fear she had. He was happy she'd opened up as much as she had. Knowing the intensity of this paralyzing fear was a major advantage. He'd now be better prepared to help her with her fear and to avoid situations that could spark hysterics. But as she continued to tremble in his arms, he wished he could simply console her for the remainder of the flight.

Gentle sobs shook her as he passed his fingers through her hair. Feeling helpless, he simply held her while murmuring soothing words.

For a man who'd known such heartache, he could certainly understand the difficulties of letting go of a long ago ghost. He knew all too well how fear could cling to a soul, how the desolation and hunger of a child constantly left a man's belly feeling in need of nutrients. Those years of loneliness before finding his nana could have scarred him so much more than they had. So what had happened in

Taryn's childhood to make such a horrific nightmare cling to her to the point of affecting her so physically?

She seemed completely unaware as New York's skyscrapers came into view. She didn't bat an eye as the plane made its descent to the airport. And when passengers got up, collected their carry-ons, Tar remained immobile. Errol had to physically pull her out of her seat and guide her off the plane.

"Do you need some medical assistance," the conscientious flight attendant asked.

Errol shook his head. "She'll be all right as soon as I can get her home. Thank you."

As they waited for their luggage, he called to have his sports car brought around.

"I don't have any luggage," Tar droned as she stood at his side. "I only had the carry-on."

Startled to hear her speak after a prolonged and tortured silence, Errol looked at her. "Tar, you feeling okay now?"

"I want to go home, Errol."

"It won't be long. I'll get my bags and I'll bring you straight to Sam's."

He mentally set aside the plans he'd had for them. After such a long and tense flight, he longed to curl up with her in bed. He longed to hold her tight, to feel her skin against his, to kiss every inch of flesh, but his carnal need of her would have to wait.

As he waited for his luggage to make its way down the conveyor belt, Tar leaned heavily into him and he could feel her exhaustion. The weekend had been difficult and she was now paying the price. Hopefully being home would have her back to her cheerful self in no time.

With his luggage in hand, he led her out to his car.

"Do you think your mom will still be at Sam's?" he asked, not so much because he needed to know, but just to keep her talking and awake.

"I'm sure she is. Unless she really had a difficult weekend. She said she was feeling better these days."

He drove through the familiar streets of New York, directing his sleek sports car to safe and familiar ground for Tar. The moment he turned into her neighborhood, she perked up, her eyes brightened and the darkness of her nightmares left her.

"It's good to be home," he offered.

She turned to him and smiled as she laid her hand over his on the stick shift. "I'm sorry I've been so difficult."

He shrugged. "Easy is boring. You're a challenge, and I love it."

Another few turns and he pulled up in front of the restaurant. Errol couldn't help but note the stark contrast between his high end design and state of the art restaurants and the older model brick and mortar restaurant that had seen little change over the years. The sign baring Taryn's mother's name was at least fifteen years old and as he followed Tar inside, he guessed the furnishings weren't much newer.

The numerous patrons, however, didn't seem to mind at all. They were completely enamored with the delicious food on their plates and the animated conversations emphasized the conviviality of the restaurant. It was the type of place that attracted people who wanted to have good food with good friends and enjoy a good time. The scents and sounds that filled the air made him wish he was seated at one of the tables. He considered some of the haute cuisine restaurants he'd been to over the years; where food was artfully plated, the ingredients pricey and rare, and the patrons often times quiet and stiff. Maybe he should consider a blend of great food with a warmer atmosphere for his next restaurant.

Sam's exuded a warmth and comfort he'd never experienced before; a sense of coming home, and as they made their way toward the back of the restaurant the sense of warmth filled him. The moment he heard Sam's voice coming from the kitchen, giving orders to his Benicoise crew, he knew where that warmth and comfort came from. Even as she bossed the crew around, she did so with a calm, generous and respectful hand. She made herself clear without being condescending, as many top chefs, including himself, were guilty of. She had her needs met without belittling her employees. She made them feel like part of the family as opposed to a paid worker.

"Mom," Tar called out as she made a beeline for the kitchen.

Glancing at Tar, he realized he felt that same warmth and comfort with her, although there was something notably different.

Bobby, donning a chef's jacket and hat, was busy at a workstation whisking the contents of the bowl in his hand. Impressed by the young man's growth since first meeting him, Errol smiled. Seemed the young Casanova really knew his way around the kitchen, something that hadn't been evident when Errol had lectured Bobby's class.

"Tar!" Sam shouted as she spotted her daughter. Turning her back to her crew, she hurried to Tar and pulled her into her arms. "What are you doing back so soon? I thought you were going to spend the week in Paris."

"I told you I wouldn't leave you alone for that long." Tar pulled back enough to look into her mother's eyes. "Besides, I already missed you."

Sam's warm laughter filled the kitchen. "Right… in Paris with your new boyfriend and you're eager to come home to your old ma. Care to tell me another story?" She glanced beyond Tar and noticed Errol. "Oh, I see."

"Hello, Mrs…"

"Sam." She held out her hand for a handshake, then pulled Errol in for a hug. "I didn't know you were coming back with Tar."

"Hey, what are you guys doing here?" Bobby called, still whisking away.

"Hey, Chef Bobby," Tar said.

Beaming with pride, Bobby whisked even faster.

"See," Sam said. "There was no reason for you to rush back. Bobby's trying out his new culinary talents on my patrons. I've had more help this weekend than I know what to do with."

"Well, I'm happy to be back all the same."

With a flourish, Bobby put the finishing touches to his dish and popped it in the oven. "Did you leave the most romantic city in the world to come home and watch your baby brother make it big in the culinary world?"

"Word of your *boeuf en croute* made it all the way to Paris and I had to rush back to taste it," she teased.

Bobby jutted his chest out, but glared as he saw Errol. "You brought your French toast back with you?"

"Bobby," Sam quickly reprimanded.

"What?" he said defensively. "Something must have happened to make her come back so quick and just look…" He pointed at Errol's face. "Look at the guilt written all over his face."

"Bobby!" Tar spat.

"Sorry. No offence, but a guy's gotta watch out for his women." He put a protective arm around his mother.

"Hey," Errol said with a chuckle. "I can understand you wanting to protect your sister."

While the kitchen bustled with hectic activity, the foursome was suddenly cloaked in uncomfortable silence for what seemed an eternity.

Why did Bobby insist on being so mistrustful? Did Taryn's entire family have issues of trust? They should know by now just how much he loved her. She should know he would never do anything to hurt her. Grinding his teeth, he tried to find the words that would convince them he was trustworthy. God, there wasn't anything he wouldn't do for Taryn. She had his heart.

It was hard to believe that only his old reputation was responsible and the more he thought about it, the more he suspected an outside influence. And just as the name of that outside influence came to him, Matt walked in.

Of course, Errol thought. Matt, the old friend, the friendly fireman, the ever present, reliable gentleman… and judging by the hungry look in his eyes, the man who wanted very much to win the heart of Taryn Cummings at all costs.

What had the nice looking and somewhat insipid fireman said to Taryn in his absence. More than anyone Errol knew the stories a man could spin when he wanted to woo a woman. A few conquests of his past had been won by spreading an unfavorable word about a rival.

All's fair in love…, he thought wryly as he set a possessive arm around Taryn's shoulders and smiled as amiably as he could considering the dislike he harbored for the young man.

"Tar!" Matt exclaimed as he rushed to Tar, and despite Errol's possessive hold, he picked her up and squeezed her in a bear hug as he twirled her around.

"When did you get back? I thought you were gone for a week or so." He put her down and looked longingly into her eyes.

"You know I can't stay away from Sam's too long." Taryn smiled up at handsome firefighter giving her lovelorn puppy dog eyes, which Errol nearly wanted to poke out.

Matt gave her a chaste kiss on the cheek, but, chaste or not, Errol stepped in and pulled Tar to his side. His lips parted with the intention of reminding the young man that Taryn was his fiancé, but he pressed them tightly together and remained silent.

"Or is it that things didn't go as planned in Paris?"

"Matt!" Tar said. "How can you say that when Errol is standing right in front of you?"

"Right," Matt said, shoving his fingers through his hair. "Nice of you to bring Tar all the way back home."

Errol nodded and muttered, "Of course."

"After all, it appears you have a rather busy schedule, being a world class chef with his own cooking show. It mustn't be easy for you to get away and take proper care of the ones you love."

While the words might have seemed innocent enough on another person's lips, Errol understood the venom behind the calmly spoken words. Squeezing Tar against him, he grinned. "I'll do whatever it takes to make my beautiful fiancé happy… happy and secure."

Far from returning Errol's forced grin, Matt's hard glare remained steady as he crossed his arms and parted his powerful legs in a stance that spoke volumes about his feelings about Errol and his fiancé.

Errol's gaze traveled quickly over Matt's oversized biceps and strong stance. Rarely given to moments of inferiority, he gritted his teeth as he considered the time a fire fighter had to work out and keep in shape whereas his profession had him standing at a counter and tasting rich and creamy dishes.

"Well, I certainly hope you'll keep her wellbeing in mind regardless of the work schedule you have."

"Taryn means the world to me and I'll make sure she knows it every single day."

Tar looked from one contemptuous man to the other. "Okay, so now that my happiness has been taken care of for all time…" She nodded at Matt while tugging at Errol. "I have a few suitcases to unpack and I want to relax and get settled in."

"Rough flight?" Matt asked.

"Yeah, you look like hell," Bobby injected. "I heard jetlag could be rough, but… maybe a nice long nap and hot shower will set you right."

Tar shot him a playfully irritated glance. "Actually, the flight was fine and I had plenty of sleep, but thanks for the suggestion all the same. Truth is, I just want to get home."

"Hey, don't shoot the messenger. I'm just trying to give you a heads-up. I mean, you're a good looking girl, even if you are my sister, but even you need freshening up every now and then. Take it from me, men want their woman to look and act like a lady… and smell like one, too. Unshaved armpits might be the big thing on the other side of the pond, but here… you've got to keep your looks up."

"Thanks, little brother."

"As it turns out, Bobby, I happen to love Taryn's womanly scents and all, just the way she is. There is nothing sexier than a woman who smells like a woman. When you love a woman, really love her, you love every scent that comes with her. That's the real chemistry. When you meet that right woman and fall in love, you'll not only love all those special scents that are just hers, but you'll crave them." He lovingly pinched Tar's cheek. "Besides, I think she looks radiant when her hair is disheveled and she has no make-up on fresh in the morning when she gets up."

Matt swallowed uncomfortably and grimaced.

Grinning, as if happy to have learned a new life and love lesson, Bobby grinned. "Whatever you say, Master Chef. I'll put the old schnozzle to work the next time I'm out with the ladies… anything to be as successful as a Master Chef like you."

"Dream big, young man. You never know how far you can go."

"Yeah," Matt muttered to himself.

Errol ignored him. "Maybe I could even give you a hand, Bobby."

"That'd be great."

"We'll get together some time and make a game plan. Your future could be even brighter than you imagine."

"And my love life?"

"Oh, Bobby," Tar said with a chuckle. "Bye, Mom. I'll see you later." She turned to Matt. "Nice seeing you, Matt."

"Sure," Matt said. "I'll see you again soon."

"Don't wait up for us," Errol called over his shoulder as he led the way out.

Once in his car, he turned the car toward his penthouse.

"I wanted to go home, Errol," Tar argued.

"And that's exactly where we're going."

# Chapter 15

## Taryn

She knew there was no point arguing with him. Truth was, she was eager to be alone with him. The events of the day had worn her out and she was in dire need of escape, and she knew Errol's expert touch would erase everything she'd been through.

They entered the building with tense silence while the electricity passed from one to the other. They hadn't even touched yet and her every nerve ending was on fire. Though the flight had been endless and painful, one bright moment shined through it all. Of course Errol had been thoughtful and tender, but at that very moment, what struck her was the sensations she'd felt while she'd slumbered. In the haze of her panic attack, she'd distinctly felt Errol's roaming hand as he'd innocently consoled her. Repeatedly his hand had slipped into her shirt to fondle a breast under cover of the darkness that had enveloped the plane.

At first the sensation entered her consciousness through vague waves of eroticism that invaded her dreams, but as his thumb had run circles around her nipple, a shock of excitement had coursed down to her thighs.

Now, as they entered the elevator, the sensations of his thumb over her nipple returned to her, reminding her that her erotic dream had been halted when the lights had turned back on and she'd stirred to full wakefulness.

The elevator doors slid shut and they stood side by side for a second, staring hungrily at each other. Just as she prepared to throw herself at him, he grabbed her and pressed her to the mirrored wall. His lips clasped over her mouth, sucking her in and devouring her with a hunger he'd never displayed before.

As the elevator rose, so did her arousal. Errol pressed his hips against hers, showing her just how aroused he was. His hardened shaft pressed into her and she let out a pleasurable groan.

"I'll make you forget that nightmare of a flight soon enough." He kissed her neck and trailed down between her breasts. "Let all your tension out, Tar and enjoy the moment."

She pulled away slightly. "Let's just wait until we get to your place," the logical side of her brain commanded.

"Afraid we'll get caught?" he teased.

"Think of your reputation, Errol. If one of your…" She let out a long, slow hiss of breath as his lips found a nipple. Breathing heavily, she continued. "… your neighbors… What if they… Ah! Errol. What will they think?"

"Any woman who comes upon us will think 'lucky girl,' and any guy who sees us…"

Suddenly the thought of getting caught added to her arousal; the thought of being seen, of being watched was arousing. She almost wished the doors would slide open. Perhaps a group of young men would stand there and gawk at them.

"Loosen up, Tar. Let go and lose yourself in the sensations of your body. Stop thinking and just feel," he said as he passed his tongue over her nipple. "Feel it and let the tension go."

"Oh, it's gone, Errol. You've already succeeded," she murmured. "And now all I want is your cock deep inside me. I want to ride you, Errol. I want to feel you."

He jacked her skirt up and ran his finger over her swollen lips. The thin fabric of her panties was too much of a barrier and she longed to have his fingers directly on her. She wanted skin on skin contact, but he continued to tease her for another excruciating moment.

"Errol," she whispered.

Hearing the full weight of his hushed name, he pulled the panties aside and ran his finger through the moisture that'd accumulated. "Yes, oh Baby, that's more like it," he groaned as he brought the moistened finger to his lips. "You certainly let go. You're even hornier than I am… and considering the stiff hard-on I have, that's saying a lot."

Narrowing his eyes with hunger, he grabbed each panel of her shirt and tore it apart then attacked the front clasp of her bra. With an expert flick of his fingers, he released her breasts.

Once again the thought of strangers watching them aroused her. Her full breasts perked and her nipples stood erect in anticipation of all to come. She opened her eyes and caught their reflection in one of the mirrors. They made for an exquisitely erotic picture.

Errol plunged between her breasts, licking, sucking, and kissing with his lips while grasping with both hands. To see him, one would think he'd never seen a pair of breasts before.

The elevator came to a stop, and in her foggy mind, she heard the doors slide open and imagined the expression on the faces of those who watched. They were shocked, but unable to pry their eyes away. They were flabbergasted, but enticed. They were aroused and eager to see more. Instead of her usual course of action, becoming inhibited and wanting to stop, she became more wanton and all sensible thought abandoned her. She arched her back and threw her head back, giving Errol even more access to her breasts all while allowing the onlookers a glimpse of the aroused orbs.

With a wild need to fulfill every sense, she pulled Errol's shirt open and kissed his chest, quickly bringing her lips to the waist of his slacks. Moving with rushed and impatient speed, she unzipped his pants and freed his erection, holding it with a tight grip.

"You want a taste?" Errol said as he teasingly pulled back.

She leaned into him, refusing to allow his cock to escape her. With hungry lips, she kissed the tender tip and he moaned his pleasure.

"Take it all in."

Holding back, she continued to kiss the very tip of his erection. "I'm not sure you deserve it."

He drove his fingers through her hair and pulled her head closer to his crotch. "Damn it, take it all in. Suck hard until I tell you to stop."

She shook her head and licked the length of his shaft, well aware of the open elevator door.

"Do you love me, Errol?" she whispered.

"Yes! Forever."

"Do you deserve me?"

"I'll prove it to you every day."

She took in a full inch of his cock.

"Ah, Lord have Mercy." His fingers tightened around her head and he rammed the full length of his cock into her mouth.

Tar welcomed him, sucking on him, licking him and pulling up on the rigid shaft, delighting in the soft and sensual feel of her tongue along his cock until he groaned deep within his chest a primal groan that shook his entire body. Knowing how she affected him, aroused her more, and she eagerly took him in deeper, sucking harder.

With a quick and harsh motion, Errol pulled her up, spun her around and pushed her head forward as he poked his cock along the moistened folds of skin.

"I wanted to keep this until later, but you're driving me crazy. I can't hold off." He plunged deep inside her from behind, rocking her hard as he thrust in and out of her frantically. "Look what you do to me, Taryn." He slapped against her, the sound of their colliding bodies filling the small space of the elevator. He gritted his teeth and exhaled, "I can't get enough of you."

She heard a gasp and wondered if it'd come from Errol or one of the onlookers. Either way, she groaned with pleasure and swung her hips from side to side in a provocative manner.

Errol reached around her, and while his cock probed her innermost core, his fingers delved through her lips and clitoris, massaging the tiny little nub to the edge of an explosive orgasm.

"You want it?" Errol asked, never stopping the motion of his cock or fingers.

"Yes," she whispered.

"You want it now?"

"Yes!" she shouted as the waves of pleasure reached an ultimate high and hovered there waiting… waiting… waiting… until. "Yes!"

Errol pounded into her just as her orgasm shook her entire body. Groaning his own climax, he straightened her up, leaned into her, and pushed her flat up against the mirrored wall as he pumped into her, pouring every last drop of him into her.

The cool glass, in sharp contrast to the heat of the moment, brought her sensations full circle. After a day that had begun, so many hours ago, with the dreaded notion that Errol was duplicitous, she was now entirely fulfilled and satisfied… and eager for more.

Suddenly mindful of the open elevator door, she turned to find the corridor empty.

"I thought we had an audience," she remarked as she looked over her shoulder at Errol.

"Are you disappointed?" he said with an amused grin. "If that's your scene, I could make arrangements next time."

She chuckled. "Now that blood is flowing freely to my brain again, I have to say no."

"But in the moment, you were thrilled by it, weren't you?"

"I wouldn't say…"

"Weren't you?" he insisted as he pulled out of her and turned her completely around. "You little vixen. I knew you were wild, but…"

"Don't get any ideas in that head of yours."

"You thought the doors could open up on any floor and expose us to strangers innocently waiting to take the elevator."

"Maybe…" she hinted. "Didn't you?"

"No," he said with a bold laugh. "I happen to know this elevator is private and only opens onto the penthouse."

Now that the erotic fog had been lifted, she remembered, rather sheepishly, that very fact. "Oh, yeah. I forgot."

Biting his lower lip, he looked at her with new awe and interest. "I never would have thought you had it in you to be so bold and abandoned…"

"Stop looking at me like that Errol. I wasn't turned on by the imaginary crowd at the elevator doors."

"A crowd, huh?" he said with increased interest.

She playfully slapped his arm and walked out of the elevator. "Cut it out. I was just caught up in the moment."

"If anything, I'd say that imaginary crowd is what had you so particularly hot and sweaty." He looked down at his aroused crotch. "Look at me. I am hard for you again just thinking about it."

Tar laughed. "You're just plain horny… no matter what you think about."

He followed her into the living room, his hands outstretched to grab her butt.

"Stop it, Errol. You've had your fun. Now I need to go wash up and get rested."

Taking a firm hold of her wrist, he pulled her back to him, her breasts colliding with his chest. "I'll give you a reason to wash up," he said, the full intent of his words clearly written across his face.

With her shirt open and her breasts barely concealed, she was alluring and enticing… and horny.

"Errol, I'm already a mess as it is."

He pushed her back onto the sofa. "Pull open your shirt," he ordered.

She slowly, ever so slowly, pulled the fabric back just to the edge of each nipple.

"More," he commanded.

Instead of opening her shirt wider, she ran her fingers along the edge of the fabric, reveling in the sensation of her firm round breasts.

"You like your tits just as much as I do," he noted. He grabbed a hold of his hard erection and aimed it at her.

"Just as much as you like your cock." Tar pulled back her shirt and grabbed both breasts, filling her tiny hands with the firm and eager flesh.

"Perk up your nipples."

She pinched and tweaked her nipples and as a shot of arousal quickly made its way to her thighs, she set both feet on the coffee table behind Errol, on either side of him.

"Sweet siren," he said as he gazed down at her exposed crotch. His fist tightened around his shaft.

While one hand remained on her breast, her other hand traveled down her belly between her legs. Running her fingers along the titillated smooth skin, she parted her lips, thoroughly enjoying the moment.

Errol edged closer, pumping harder and faster.

Knowing it would drive him to the edge, Tar brought both hands to her crotch and pulled the tender, moistened folds of skin apart, showing Errol just how aroused she was.

"Damn it, Tar," he hissed as his eyes narrowed.

For several moments she simply ran her fingers around and around the soft skin, her eyes never leaving his. His gaze riveted to the motions of her fingers, it was as if nothing else existed.

"Go in," he whispered hoarsely.

"I'm not ready yet."

He inhaled with difficulty and let the air slowly seep between his lips. His jaw was slack in concentration and his gaze never wavered from her fingers.

"Please," he said. "Go in, now. I can't…"

Eager to please him and herself, she nudged her finger deep inside the warmth and moisture. "Like this?"

"Ah, shit."

Pulling out to dive back in, she mimicked the motions of intercourse.

"Ah, shit!"

"Don't make a mess, Errol," she said with matron authority.

"Yes."

"Errol, don't!" she commanded with a secret smile.

"Yes!" He set one hand on the sofa's armrest and groaned his release.

"Errol!" she shouted with mock anger.

Gently squeezing out the last drops of his arousal, he grinned at her. "You continue to surprise me, my lovely Taryn."

"As do you, Errol. As do you."

He cupped her chin and pulled her mouth to his where he savagely kissed her, plunging his tongue into her mouth to tangle with hers. "I hunger for you," he said. "Go, take your shower, but we're not through yet."

She couldn't take her eyes off his lips and his burning eyes. They've just had the most passionate raw sex, yet she couldn't get enough of him. Errol King was sex incarnate. Everything about him radiated it. He was insatiable.

"You can literally have whatever you want now." He took her hand and helped her up. "Come on. Let's get you washed up."

In the bathroom, he turned on the shower and they hopped into the stall.

"Sure feels good," Errol said as he dunked under the flow of water.

Tar took her time washing, reveling in the warm water. When she stepped out the phone rang.

"You want me to get that?" Tar offered as Errol remained under the flow of water.

"Naw. I'm not expecting anything important. It'll go to voicemail."

Tar grabbed a towel just as the caller got to the voicemail.

"Errol. Errol are you there?" a female voice asked.

Tar almost doubled over as the wind was knocked out of her at the sound of that seductive and husky tone.

"Errol, pick up. I absolutely have to talk to you," she insisted with a guttural laugh.

After a long pause she went on. "Well, I heard you were home in New York, that'd you'd taken a flight in from Paris. Look, if rumors are true and you are in New York, I would really, really like to see you. Thing is, I've just had my place remodeled and I think it looks just fabulous. I'd really like to have you take a look at it, tell me what you think. You know how I appreciate your opinion."

Frozen to the spot, Tar listened with growing nausea.

"Of course, my apartment isn't the only thing I want you to take a look at. It just so happens that I spent the better part of the afternoon at this new little lingerie boutique and I have a few adorable little outfits I'd like to show you. I know how you love violet and I think you'll love the stunning lace bra and garters I got."

Tar gagged as Errol pulled away from the flow of water, wiped the water from his face and heard the ongoing message.

"And if you don't like that one," she went on, "I also bought this kinky little number that is sure to get you excited."

"I think I'll have to go get that." Errol shut the water off and moved to step out of the shower, but Tar blocked his path.

"I want to hear it." Stone-faced, Tar stood her ground.

"It's been over a month since I've seen you," the cool female voice said. "and I'm really starting to miss you. You know our last night together was so hot, I mean, honey, you were on fire, and you left me steaming for weeks, but now I'm ready to steam it up again. Give me a call and let your sugar baby share her warmth with you, sweetie. You have my number. Call any time. I'm up until late."

"Tar," Errol said as he pushed past her.

"What? Are you going to tell me that was a wrong number?" she spat.

Tight-lipped, he shook his head.

"Who was that, Errol?"

"That's not important."

"No, you're right. It's not important. What is important is that you were with some fucking girl… a month ago? You fucked some other girl a month ago? Did she really do it for you, Errol? Huh? Did she steam it up for you?

"Tar, stop it."

"Stop it? Honey, I'm just getting started. You told me running around and womanizing was a part of your past. You said it was far behind you. Sorry, Errol, but a month ago is not far behind you. That's while you knew me. That's while we were together… and that makes you a lying, cheating scumbag."

"Tar, we weren't together. Technically, we weren't. You'd left, remember? It happened when you left me high and dry in Paris to return home to America."

She huffed. "Really, Errol. You want to call this on a technicality. This isn't some freakin' game, you pig. This is a relationship. No. Scratch that. This *was* a relationship, because as far as I'm concerned, this is it… over. I've had enough. I've seen enough. And don't you dare try to sweet talk your way out of it this time, Errol, because the proof of the man you really are is right there in that voicemail. If ever you start to wonder why we didn't work out, just listen to it again and remind yourself of the pig you really are."

"You're not being fair. You'd left, Tar. You left me with no way of reaching you, of finding you."

Narrowing her eyes, she glared at him with hateful venom. She quickly patted herself dry and grabbed her clothes.

"You know what, Errol? I don't really care what you do. I don't care what you did when we broke up then, and I don't care what you do after we break up now. I just want to get dressed and I'll be out of your place and out of your life." She jerked her skirt on and struggled to get her still damp arms into her buttonless blouse. She didn't want to waste any time going through her luggage to find something more suitable and simply knotted the blouse beneath her breasts.

Errol reached for her arm. "Tar, you're making it sound like I have no feelings in all this. Do you know what it did to me to have you leave like that? I was heart-broken. And believe me, I did spend many nights wondering and worrying about you, but forgive me if I'm not the type of man who'll just roll up into a ball and cry endlessly over a break up. I got out and tried to erase the pain… yes, in another woman's bed, but only because you pushed me away. It was a mistake that I wished never happened, but I've never felt so devastated like that before. I didn't know what to do. All I knew was I wanted to erase you from my heart, to drown all my pain into something…and she was there."

"And how long did it take you to find that other woman's bed, Errol? Two days, three? Did you give it a week?"

He stared dumbly at her.

Tearing away from him, she shouted, "I thought you loved me."

"I did. I do. That's what made being without you so difficult. Damn it, Tar. I was trying to get over you; trying to move on."

"Who is it? Huh? Who's the girl? A student? A fan? A patron of your restaurant?"

His eyes veiled with guilt and the blow hit her in the gut as painfully as if he'd struck her. Swallowing her disgust, she reached for the counter to steady herself.

"It's Suzanne, isn't it?"

He remained silent and dropped his gaze to the floor.

"I can't believe it."

"Tar," he murmured.

"Of all people, you went and screwed that witch Suzanne? Damn it, Errol. Damn you!" She pounded her fists into his chest as tears of frustration streamed down her cheeks. "Damn you!"

"Honey, that was a mistake. You left me. We weren't together any longer. It meant nothing to me."

"I heard her, Errol. It didn't seem to matter little to her." Clenching her teeth, she glanced at the ceiling, wishing there was a way to erase everything that had just happened. "Why her, Errol? Damn it, of all people, why her?"

"I didn't go out looking to be with someone, Tar. She was just there."

Leaning back against the counter, the main thrust of anger dissipated and Tar was simply left with the emptiness and pain of his betrayal.

"You work with her, Errol. Even if I had a hope of ever forgiving you, how could I ever trust you, knowing that you're working with her day in and day out? What am I supposed to really think you're doing when you stay late at the restaurant night after night… all alone with her?" She shook her head with disgust. "Never. I'd never be able to trust you again…let alone marry you."

"You're not giving me much credit."

She sullenly stared straight ahead.

"Tar," he whispered as he grasped her shoulders. "You heard the message. It was over ever since I saw you at Sam's that first night I ate there. The moment I found you, the moment you allowed me into your life again, I cut ties with her. She knew that."

"Then why is she calling you. That message wasn't that of a woman who's been ditched. It's the message of a woman who expects to easily reconnect with a lover."

"That's her take on the situation, not mine. She's persistent. I told her when I was here with you in New York, that you and I are together."

Taryn couldn't get Suzanne's message to Errol out of her head. She closed her eyes, seeing pitch black darkness and felt her heart rate go up as the beat of her heart became louder and louder. How could she trust Errol? How could she trust Suzanne won't try to seduce him every chance she got while they "worked" together. First Madame X, the pretty girls in his class, and now Suzanne. Would it always be like this? Could she handle it? She didn't want to marry someone like her father. She didn't want to make the same mistake as her mother, marrying someone who didn't value marriage or family. She grew up watching how her mother struggled raising two kids and trying to make ends meet. She grew up without a father. As much as she loved Errol, she was frightened that he would end up like her father, having affairs and being a deadbeat. Before she could stop herself, she said, "well, here's my take on the situation, Errol. This is over."

# Chapter 16

Tar rushed to Errol's private elevator and repeatedly punched the button. The doors quickly slid open. Her head down in anger and pain, Tar marched into the elevator only to stop dead in her tracks as she spotted the bright red spike heels. Blinded with rage, her gaze followed up the trim line of calves and thighs, the tight black skirt that hugged dangerous curves and the unbelievably low cut shimmering yellow halter top. Just short of looking at the woman's face, Tar stopped, not wanting to see, not wanting to know.

Trying desperately to control her anger, she finally looked straight into Suzanne's face. She couldn't help but notice the pleased and victorious smile on the vile woman's lips. The witch didn't even seem surprised to see her there. And where had she called from? The lobby?

The rage finally took over and Tar lunged at Suzanne, slapping the witch's grin right off her face. But while Suzanne winced for a brief moment, a self-satisfied and devious grin quickly curved her lips as she walked out of the elevator and turned back to Tar just as the doors slid shut.

Tar wanted to scream, wanted to throw herself against the elevator walls, wanted to crumble to the floor and cry. The witch! Trembling with rage, she watched the numbers count down the floors that passed. As the fourth floor was counted off, Tar realized she'd have to call a cab to get home. As the third floor was counted off, she reached for her purse to pull out her phone only to realize she'd left it at Errol's. And as the second floor was counted off, she realized she didn't have a dime on her, no credit cards, not identification… nothing. She'd left everything up in Errol's apartment.

"Damn!" she shouted into the empty elevator.

As she reached the ground floor and the doors slid open, she knew she had to go back up. It was the last thing she wanted to do… to face Suzanne again… to see her fawn over Errol… and worse still, to see Errol welcome her into his arms.

For a long moment she stared out from the elevator. If she stepped out and the doors closed behind her, she wouldn't be able to get back in without a key… and just as that thought struck her, she noted that Suzanne must have had a key in order to take the elevator up.

"Ha!" she huffed. "The relationship is over… my ass."

She punched the "close door" button and prepared for the confrontation to come. Her heart pounded and her breath came fast and short.

Just as the elevator reached Errol's floor, Tar heard his hushed voice as he spoke to Suzanne. Unable to make out a word, she was nonetheless shocked by the soft and affectionate tone he used with her. She shouldn't be surprised, after all they'd been lovers, but still, to hear him stung more than she could have imagined. Though she was well aware it would be torture, she held her breath and leaned into the "close door" button to keep the door from opening at his floor. Leaning into the wall as tears streamed down her face, she pressed her forehead to the mirror, willing herself to find the strength to push the "open door" button and get her things and get out of his life for good.

Biting her lip, she brought her finger to the button, but it just hovered there, unable to press.

"I was in the neighborhood and I thought I'd drop by. It's not as if I haven't done it before," Suzanne purred.

"Things have changed, Suzanne," Errol said. "I thought I'd made that clear. I'm serious about Taryn. We're engaged and I take that very seriously."

"Really? Come on, Errol. I know you, remember? I know the kind of man you are… really are. This whole engagement thing is a real joke."

"I changed. I grew up. I fell in love. Need I go on?"

"You've fallen into a slump. You're feeling old and in need of security. You're infatuated with a silly little girl. Need *I* go on?"

"Stop it."

"Ah, come on. Loosen up."

"Suzanne," he growled. "I said stop it."

Even from inside the security of her elevator, Tar shuddered at the anger that reverberated from him and inadvertently pressed on the "open door" button. The doors slid open and with one foot still in the elevator and the other in the entry hall of Errol's penthouse, Tar held her breath and watched the lovers' quarrel.

Errol gripped Suzanne's wrist, but there was no eroticism, no passion, no affection… just pure fury and the dire need to get rid of her.

"I want you to leave here and I want you to forget my phone number," he said.

"Errol, you can't be serious. Think of the last night that we spent together. We were so hot, so on fire, so in tune to one another."

"You know, I hate to break it to you, but… thing is, I don't really remember the last time we were together. In fact, I remember little of the last few times we've been together. I was drunk and depressed."

Suzanne's jaw dropped and her eyes narrowed.

"You see, the thing is," he went on, painfully driving the point home. "Every time I was with you, I was thinking of her. Every time I touched you, I imagined I was touching her, and every time I looked at you, it was her that I saw. I know you don't want to believe it, Suzanne, but I really do love Taryn, and I want her."

"Liar!" she spat. "That skinny little bitch can't possibly keep you happy like…"

"Suzanne, you're making this more difficult than it needs to be, but, truth is, you leave me no choice. I can't possibly work with someone who so blatantly disregards my wishes. I can't work with someone who'll continually threaten my marriage."

Stomping her foot and clenching her fists, she glared at him. "What are you saying?"

"I think you know what I'm saying."

"I want to hear you say it. I want to hear the words from your lips."

"Suzanne, why are you doing this?"

"Say it!"

"You leave me no choice, but to relieve you of your duties."

"You're firing me? I, who have put so much work into building *your* restaurant, into making it one of the most talk about spots in New York. Do you know how many offers I've had recently? Dozens, and I've refused them all to stay and help you build La Benicoise into what is it, and you're just going to throw all that away... and for what? "

"You're making it impossible not to, Suzanne. I don't want to have to let you go, but I can't trust that you won't pull this sort of thing again."

"You're firing me?" she shouted. Enraged, she turned to the elevator and spotted Tar. "Because of that little bitch!"

Shocked by the whole scene, Tar stood motionless as Suzanne marched toward her. Even as the angry woman raised her hand to strike her, she didn't move to protect herself. The sting of her hand left her stunned and staring as Suzanne stomped into the elevator.

"You'll regret this, Errol King," Suzanne screamed. "You'll regret the day you chose her over me."

Tar stepped out in time to watch the doors slide shut and the apartment fell silent.

"Tar," Errol said after a stunned moment. "You came back. Are you okay?"

"Yeah," Taryn said, looking down. "Other than a little sting, I'm okay." After a while, she looked into his eyes and said, "I heard your argument with Suzanne."

For a long moment he looked at her, not quite understanding.

"I forgot all my stuff and had to come back," she explained.

"Oh," he muttered as he shifted uneasily.

"Look, I'm sorry about running out. I… it hurt to think… You… with her. I thought you were cheating on me, but I can understand how our split could… Well, I don't like the thought of you with her, but I can understand how you could. I mean, you couldn't know that we would ever see each other again. I guess I shouldn't have ignored all your messages. Maybe if I had given you a glimpse of hope, all this wouldn't have happened."

"And I'm sorry I ever got involved with Suzanne in the first place. I should have known she'd be trouble. Does that tell you just how bleak the situation was after you left? It'd been a long time since I'd felt so abandoned… not since Nana passed away. I think I was more devastated than even I realized. I must have been to have fallen into Suzanne's trap." He looked sheepishly at Tar. "And I have to admit, I was a little upset with you. I think a part of me wanted to hurt you just like you'd hurt me."

Surprised by how calm and at peace she felt, Tar nodded her understanding. She couldn't' go on blaming him when she'd had a part in the whole ordeal. As much as she hated the thought of him in that woman's arms, she knew she had to move past it if they were ever to survive as a couple. "The important thing is that it's over now. I think she finally got the message. And I think we'll be able to move on from now on."

Errol looked like he couldn't believe his eyes. "I'm happy to hear that."

"But just so we're clear, I do have a pretty mean jealous streak… added to that, I can wield a pretty mean set of kitchen knives."

Errol smiled for the first time. "I know. You have fantastic knife skills."

# Chapter 17

Tar glanced at her watch as she prepared to close Sam's for the night. It was almost midnight and she had an hour to clean up and get ready for the next morning before Errol arrived.

After a few days away from Sam's it felt good to be back in the swing of things, but the long days drained her energy. Errol's crew continued to be a blessing and although Bobby had already left earlier that night, he'd been on the ball since early that morning. With Sam taking a well-deserved night off, Tar and Bobby had directed Errol's crew with precision and efficiency.

Now all that remained were a few wipe downs here and there and some last minute preparations for the following day's menu. She jotted down on a slip of paper the few items she already knew she was low on.... fresh lettuce, tomatoes, cream and blue cheese. She headed to the oversized pantry, and twisted and turned the combination on the lock... 15 to the right, 42 to the left and 2 to the right. She yanked it off and pulled open the heavy door. Though not a refrigerated room, it was nonetheless closed off from the heat of the kitchen and managed to remain cool at all times.

She grabbed the yard long stick leaning in the corner just outside the pantry and propped one end of it under the crossbar of the door and the other in a small dent in the cement floor to hold the door open. Walking in, she flicked on the light.

The shelves, lined with a few canned goods, many dry items like flour, sugar and rice, and crates of fresh fruits and vegetables, ran up to the ceiling. Most were full, but the shelf of fresh herbs was a little low. As she bent down to look at the contents of the many containers, she jotted down the needed herbs; rosemary, thyme and although the container of sage was half full, she knew it went down fast and jotted it down as well.

Hearing footsteps in the kitchen, she didn't look up, but called out, "Bobby, is that you?"

No response, but the footsteps approached.

Smiling, she called out, "Errol?" Perhaps he'd decided to come pick her up earlier than agreed upon.

Still no response. She hurriedly jotted down the last item for her list and was about to set her pen and paper down when a loud rattling sound startled her. The stick that held the door open, she thought. It must have fallen.

She tossed her things onto the shelf and hurried to the door just as it slammed shut.

"Hello," she shouted through the dense wood as she tried to push it open. "Is somebody there? Open the door!"

She heard a strange scraping sound than the distinct sound of the latch being thrown onto the door.

"Wait!" she screamed as she pounded on the door.

The combination lock was settled into place and clamped shut.

"Hey!" Her screams were now those of a nearly hysterical woman. "I'm in here."

She pressed her ear to the door and listened. Other than a low rumbling sound, she heard nothing. Leaning back against the door, she forced herself to calm down. She had to think rationally. She had to conserve her energy. First things first. At the very back of the large pantry was a small window. With calm and purposeful steps she hurried to the back of the pantry, pushed a few boxes under the window and climbed up.

The window hadn't been opened in ages and latch was old and rusted. Unable to unlock it with her bare hands, she hopped off the boxes and rummaged through a crate of old utensils they no longer used but that her mother insisted on keeping. With an old pair of crab pliers, she climbed back up and forced the latch open.

She hurriedly threw the window open, but just before she could sigh her relief at the abundant fresh air that came in, the lights went out and she was left in total darkness.

"Calm," she said aloud. "Everything that was there a minute ago in the light, is still right where it was. Nothing has changed. Nothing has moved."

But despite her calming words of reassurance, her heart raced and her palms quickly became clammy. She climbed down from the boxes and stood still for a long moment. There was no one behind the shelf, she told herself. There's nothing hidden under the bottom shelf. There's nothing but the darkness.

She gripped the edge of her shirt, tugging and pulling as panic slowly but surely trickled into her veins, pumping her blood with adrenaline as the fear mounted. Fear of what, she didn't know, but it remained all the same, just as it always had... ever since those days...

Shaking her head she tried to keep from going to that long ago place... that dark and scary place, but the child in her took the reins, bringing her back to the many times she'd been locked in a closet.

Her father; she remembered little of him and what little memories remained were all bad, fearful even. His drunken tirades were the most vivid. And then there were his many fights with her mother; fights that went beyond loud arguments about money and gambling and drinking; fights that usually ended with Sam bruised and in tears while her father ran off to drink or gamble some more.

Tar closed her eyes and tried to shut out the awful images that rushed to her. She pushed the memories back so far, always refusing to acknowledge them, always refusing to allow them to come forth, to explain her fear to her.

But now it rushed full force, the last times she'd been locked up, and she couldn't escape it. One drunken night while Sam worked late to provide for her family what her father couldn't, he'd made a clumsy attempt at making dinner; macaroni and cheese, but instead of adding milk as the box instructed, he'd poured a bottle of beer into the mix.

"This isn't very good, Daddy," Taryn had said as politely as she could.

Across the table from her, Bobby had sat silently staring into the disgusting pasta.

"What did you say?" her father had bellowed.

"Nothing, Daddy." She'd tried to force down a huge forkful, but gagged and spit it back into her bowl. "I'm sorry, Daddy. I don't like beer. I can't," she said with a shaky voice.

"You ignorant and ungrateful brat." He grabbed her by the wrist, yanked her out of her chair and dragged her to the linen closet by the back door.

"No," she shouted and she tried to wring free, but she only succeeded in angering him more, pushing him to squeeze tighter on her tiny wrist.

She glanced up at Bobby and saw the horror in his tear filled eyes.

Her father opened the linen closet and shoved her inside.

"No, Daddy. Please don't," she begged as she crouched down under the shelf of towels. "I'll eat it, Daddy. I promise. I'll eat it all. Please..."

He slammed the door shut and hooked the latch that Sam had put in several weeks before to keep Bobby from going in the closet to play with bathroom cleaning products.

For an hour Tar sat on the floor, her feet amidst the scouring powders, window washing liquids and other chemicals that kept the house clean. She'd long ago given up calling and begging her father to come open the door.

She'd long ago stopped staring at the line of light that came in from under the door, hoping to see the shadow that would be her father coming to let her out.

But as she heard her father carry Bobby off to bed and prepare for another night out drinking and gambling, her calls for release began anew. They were quickly silenced, however, when the kitchen light was switched off and she heard the front door slam shut.

In complete darkness a whole new fear set in. Imaginary spiders crept out from every crevice. Monsters that could seep in through the bottom of the door came to her child's eye. Shocked silent, she simply stared straight ahead as her body numbed. She hid inside herself, deep, so deep that no monster would ever find her.

The hours dragged on and she dozed off, her dreams bombarded with impossible creatures that filled the darkness. When, in the wee hours of the morning, she heard the distant voice of her mother, Tar opened her eyes and saw the ray of light that beamed in from under the door. It was morning.

"Mom," she called, her voice coming out thick and raspy from her dry throat.

The door opened, and while blinded by the bright morning light, Taryn rushed out of her holding cell and ran into her mother's arms.

"Taryn, honey, what are you doing in there?" Sam said with a lighthearted chuckle. "Were you playing hide and seek, and no one found you?"

"No," she said. She wanted to be a big girl and not cry, but the tears streamed down her face. "Daddy punished me."

"Daddy? Daddy put you in there?"

Tar nodded as Sam's cheeks turned red and her lips white. She gripped Taryn's shoulders. "I'll be back in a minute to make breakfast. Just sit here a minute." She stormed off and headed to her bedroom.

At first the voices were muffled and hard to make out, but they quickly rose in volume and intensity.

"How could you lock her up in there?" Sam shouted.

"I told you. The kid refused to eat dinner. Stop hassling me over the way I discipline my kids."

"Discipline? That's not discipline, that's child abuse. She spent the entire night in a closet."

"I just wanted to put her in there to show her a little appreciation. What kind of a kid are you raising if they can just turn their nose up at the dinner you put down on the table? You tell me."

Sam stomped back to the kitchen and picked up one of the uneaten bowls of macaroni. Bringing the pasta to her nose, she sniffed. "This is what you call dinner?"

"Hey, I never said I was like Chef Samantha. Hell, I was just trying to help."

"What the hell did you put in here, beer?"

"I don't know. I read the box. Hell if I know."

"You tried to feed the kids macaroni and cheese and beer, you idiot," she shouted then she pointed a shaky finger at Tar. "And she's the one who gets locked up for the night?"

"I didn't mean to leave her in there all night. I forgot her is all."

"Get out."

"What the hell you talking about?"

"I want you out of here. I'll give you one hour to get your stuff and get out of my house."

"Sam, I forgot her," he said with his hands in the air. "It's not like I did it on purpose."

"You got drunk, tried to feed you kids crap, locked your daughter up for no good reason and ran off to gamble my hard earned money away. I've had enough of you."

Shocked, Taryn had watched the scene with a blend of relief and guilt. After that day she never saw her father again and while she often felt responsible for that, deep down she knew it had been for the best.

As she stared into the blackness of the pantry in the restaurant her mother had worked so hard for, she remembered that horrible day and she tried to remain calm. Errol was set to pick her up within the next hour. Surely she could sit out waiting for him in the pantry. He would arrive, open the door and the whole ordeal would be over with. Just the image of his face was like a soothing balm. She had nothing to worry about. All would end well.

Her frazzled nerves found a semblance of calm until she smelled smoke. Fumbling her way in the dark she returned to the door and immediately heard the distinctive cackling of fire. Suddenly panicked, she pushed on the door, but the already intense heat kept her from touching it again.

"Help!" She shouted through the door, but knew no one was on the other side. The window, she thought. She turned to run back to the window, but slammed into the corner of one of the shelving units. Instantly, a trickle of blood ran from her forehead into her eye and on down her cheek. Patting her hand to the wound she felt the unusual amount of blood that flowed and was thankful it didn't hurt as much as it should. She reached the back of the pantry and felt around for the shelf with the small towels, grabbed one and pressed it to her forehead.

At the window, she climbed up once more and screamed out for help. Surely someone would hear her. Surely someone would see or smell the smoke.

She coughed and realized the smoke was coming in more than she'd thought. In the pitch blackness she couldn't see it, but breathing had quickly become difficult and her eyes now burned to the point of barely being able to keep them open. With the layout of the pantry clearly marked out in her head, she climbed down the boxes, grabbed as many towels off the shelf as she could and quickly but carefully returned to the door where she lay the towels out neatly over the crack under the door.

Despite her efforts, she coughed repeatedly and felt a little lightheaded. Crouching down on all fours, she brought one of the towels over her mouth and temporarily managed to catch her breath. As she crawled to the furthest corner of the pantry, she willed Errol to hurry to come pick her up. Since knowing him, he'd always been there for her; letting her stay with him when she had no place to live in Paris; helping her and her family when Sam got hurt; and now... surely he wouldn't let her down now.

Increasingly weak, she lay down on the cool cement floor with a towel draped across her face. Breathing was possible, but barely. Though she tried to remain optimistic, the dreaded outcome of this ordeal plagued her. She would not make it through the night.

"Errol," she whispered as she thought of the wonderful but short time they'd had together. She wanted so much more of life, of her time with him. "I love you, Errol King. I love you."

# Chapter 18

A loud knocking sound stirred her from her state of semi consciousness and semi sleep, then male voices shouting at one another brought her to complete wakefulness. Tar scrambled to her feet and carefully made her way to the door.

"In here!" she shouted. "I'm in here! Please, hurr..." she choked and coughed.

The pantry had become unbearably hot and it took all her will to remain upright.

"Help!" was all she could choke out.

"Tar?" a muffled voice called.

"Matt! I'm in here. I'm trapped and..." She stopped as a violent fit of coughing took over.

"Back away from the door, Tar. We're coming in."

She backed up to the window and waited.

A loud clang reverberated in the room, then another and another. Soon a small opening appeared in the door and a faint stream of fiery light entered the darkened pantry. As the firemen worked their axes through the door, more and more light came in, however an equal amount of smoke came with it.

Within minutes Tar was blinded by the smoke and simply sat on her boxes and waited with her towel over her mouth. Moments later she heard approaching footsteps.

"Tar!" Matt said through his mask. He grabbed her, slung her over his shoulder and hurried out of the pantry.

She forced her eyes open as they passed through the embers that had once been her kitchen. Matt set her down and just as quickly she was swept up into another pair of arms, this time Errol's.

"Tar," he sighed as he pulled her tightly against him. "Tar, are you all right?"

Matt pulled off his mask and set it over her face, letting her breathe clean air for a few moments. "Why don't you take her outside? They'll take a good look at her to make sure everything's okay," he suggested to Errol. "I have to go back inside."

Taryn gave him back his mask. "Thank you, Matt."

He smiled, patted her on the shoulder then slipped the mask back on before returning to the smoking kitchen.

"Come on," Errol said. "Let's get you out of here."

Outside, Sam's cozy family restaurant was bathed in a swirl of red lights coming from the many fire trucks that lined the street. Fortunately the front of the restaurant seemed unharmed by the flames, though she hated to think of the damage the smoke may have caused.

After the paramedics checked her over and gave her the okay, she walked back to the front of the restaurant with Errol. His face black with soot and ash, he smiled woefully.

"You sure gave me a scare," he said softly as he reached out to point at the bandage on her head.

"It's just a little cut. More blood than pain."

Errol sighed and pulled her into his arms.

"I don't understand," she mumbled into his chest. " I don't know what happened. I was taking inventory, just making a list of a few things I needed to pick up and... the door closed." She looked at him. "I'm so glad you came, Errol. I thought I'd never see you again. I thought you'd arrive to pick me up and I'd be..."

He kissed her brow and squeezed her against his chest. "I arrived early and saw smoke. Before I even had time to call 911, I heard the sirens." He pulled back and looked at her. "I tried to call you, but you didn't answer. I went inside and couldn't find you. I thought you'd run out. Maybe you'd gone home..."

"You couldn't have known I was locked in the pantry." Running a hand through her tangled hair, she looked into the window of Sam's. Though the flames were out, smoke from the kitchen still rose into the midnight air. "All of my mother's hard work. That kitchen..." Tears streamed down her face as she thought of the pain it would cause her mother.

"The important thing is that you're okay."

Shaking her head, she tried to make sense of it all. "Errol," she said, unsure she really wanted to voice her suspicions. "This wasn't an accident. I heard someone out in the kitchen before the door closed."

"You think this was deliberate?"

She turned at the sound of approaching footsteps. Matt, his face grim and unhappy, came to her.

"She's right. It was deliberate. She was deliberately locked inside the pantry and the fire was deliberately set."

"Isn't it a little too soon to know?"

"The surveillance tape survived and I pushed the fire inspector to take a quick look at it right away."

"You suspect foul play?" Errol said.

"Not only was the door of the panty closed, it was padlocked. That doesn't happen by accident. The only question I had was who. Who could have done such a thing?"

"And? What did you find on the tape?" Tar asked.

"A tall, statuesque woman wearing spike heels and a slinky dress. Not your usual arsonist attire, but we clearly see her closing the pantry door, putting the lock in and setting the kitchen ablaze. I'm sure she thought she was being smart when she set a shallow pan of oil on the gas burner. As you might expect, the oil bubbled over in no time, spilled over onto the open flame then quickly spread by way of the rolls of paper towels she conveniently placed overhead."

"Suzanne," Errol whispered as the very thought entered Taryn's mind.

"A friend of yours?" Matt said with a bitter tone.

Errol sneered, but said nothing.

Matt looked at Tar. "Anyway, you've got an open and shut case, not only arson, but attempted murder. Fortunately, locking you into the pantry is what saved your life in this devious plan of hers. Those walls are a foot thick and the fire would have taken hours to penetrate. As long as you managed to keep the smoke out, you were okay. And I guess her plans to get away with it didn't take into account the surveillance system you guys have."

"I can't believe it," Tar muttered. Although she knew Suzanne was desperate to get her hands on Errol again, she never would have thought her capable of something so horrific.

Matt glanced at Errol. "The footage is over there in the smaller red truck. Why don't you go have a look at it to make sure it's really who you think it is?"

Errol nodded, but seemed horrified at the prospect. Nonetheless, he left Taryn's side and headed to the truck.

"How you holding up?" Matt asked.

"Okay, I guess. I have to admit, I'm not looking forward to telling my mom about this. It'll kill her."

"Don't worry. The insurance should take care of everything. The place will be running like new again in a week or so."

She smiled and hoped he was right.

"You know, in light of what's happened here, I have to say that I may have been wrong about Errol."

"What do you mean?"

"The fire at his restaurant. I think this Suzanne person might be responsible for it after all. I didn't recognize her at first, but now that Errol mentioned it, I do remember seeing her at his restaurant that day. I thought she acted strangely, but didn't think more of it. I think I was too convinced of Errol's culpability. Anyway, I can't confirm anything just yet, but... well, it's all starting to point to her." Matt shrugged. "If so, then everything is starting to make sense."

Taryn patted his arm. "Thanks, Matt. For everything. You're a true friend."

Matt winced. "Looks like that's what I'll forever be for you, Tar. I'm just glad Errol isn't what I thought he was, otherwise it'd be even harder. But he did find you so I'm grateful he did."

Taryn reached out and wrapped her arms around Matt's thick neck. "You are really amazing, Matt. Someday, you will make some lucky girl really happy."

"I wanted that girl to be you," Matt said softly. "For years…but," he swallowed. "I know my face wasn't the face you saw right before you passed out, wasn't it?"

Taryn sadly shook her head.

"Errol?" Matt asked.

Taryn's eyes glistened with unshed tears. "Life is funny, Mattie. As much as I tried to fight it, you can't help who you fall in love with."

"Then I wish you the very best, Tar. You deserve it," Matt kissed her cheeks and hugged her before walking sadly away.

# Chapter 19

Tar sat in the dressing room of the bridal shop waiting for her dress to be brought in for a fitting. It had been a few weeks after the fire at Sam's, but she felt ready. When faced with death, the person she thought of the most, the last person she thought off before saying "good-bye" was Errol. She knew she wanted to spend the rest of her life with him then. She was certain, despite all her petty fears and insecurities before, that Errol was the man for her.

"Nervous, honey?" Sam asked as she squeezed her hand. The fire at the restaurant had barely fazed her, and news of the upcoming wedding had had her singing a merry tune for weeks.

"I just want it to be perfect," Tar said. "I want Errol to see me walking down the aisle and just go nuts for me."

"I think that's already been taken care of, sweetie."

Tar smiled just as the door opened and Hannah, the fitter, brought in her dress.

"Sorry I made you wait," Hannah said. "Here it is." She pulled the plastic wrapper off the pristine white dress and held it up for Tar to look at.

Frowning, Tar looked at the dress. "It's a lot whiter than I remember."

"The dress you tried on was probably a little yellowed. That happens a lot."

"What do you think, Mom," Tar said, turning to her mother for advice.

"Why don't you try it on, and we'll see?"

Tar pulled her simple cotton summer dress over her head and, with the aid of Hannah and her mother, squirmed into the form fitting dress.

The bodice of the simple white chiffon dress was then laced up tight.

"How's that feel?" Hannah asked.

"It could go a little tighter."

She pulled a little more. "There. How's that?"

Tar nodded and with the dress secure, turned around to face her reflection. She immediately trembled with giddiness and anticipation. "What do you think, Mom?"

With tears in her eyes, Sam nodded. "You're radiant, honey. It's absolutely perfect. Stunning."

Tar pulled her hair up atop her head and glanced sidelong at her reflection.

"You want to try on a veil?" Hannah asked.

Tar nodded and Hannah left the room.

Running her hands over the tight strapless bodice, Tar had to agree with her mother. The dress was perfect. Simple in its perfection, the only adornment were the tiny pearls sewn in. The skirt flowed to the floor with a modest train at the back. Twisting from side to side, she made the skirt swirled around her and imagined her first dance with her new husband.

"You like him, Mom?"

"Errol?"

"Yeah. I mean, I'm not rushing into this, am I?" After the fire, Errol had quickly set a date, preferring to marry her sooner rather than later.

Sam stammered for a moment then smiled. "I may have had my reservations at first, but I think he's proven just how much he loves you; just how far he'd go to make you happy."

Tar nodded. Since Suzanne had been found guilty of setting ablaze Sam's and La Benicoise, all doubts and questions about Errol's morals and ethics had been cleared. And even though La Benicoise was far from ready to re-open, Errol had put all his efforts into helping Tar and her mom open Sam's as quickly as possible. It had taken a week of hard work, but her mother's pride and joy was back on its feet and better than ever.

When word got out about the fire, their patrons rallied behind them, ready to come back to make Sam's the success it deserved to be.

"He has been wonderful, hasn't he?"

"I'll admit, when I first met him I found him arrogant, a bit cold and self-centered. I didn't think he had it in him to be so selfless. I think you bring out the best in him."

"Funny, he told me that once."

"Well then, we agree. You two are meant for one another."

Tar met her mother's gaze. "What about you and Dad?"

Sam cocked a surprised brow. "What about us?"

"Have you kept in touch over the years?"

"Not particularly, but I did run into him a few years ago. I hardly recognized him at first. He'd lost weight and seemed so much older than he should."

"You never told us."

Sam shook her head. "I didn't want to get your hopes up. I didn't want you guys to think he was ready to come back into your lives. Since then I heard he'd gotten his life back on track... he's sobered up. After he left us, after he lost everything, he ended up in a shelter and stayed there for years. Eventually he decided to get treatment for his alcoholism."

"Do you know where I could reach him?"

Cocking her head to the side, Sam reached out to finger a ringlet of hair that fell to Taryn's shoulder. "Why would you want to do that, honey?"

"I know it might not make sense, I mean considering everything that happened when I was little, but... I guess the princess in me has always dreamed of having both my parents at my wedding; of having my father walk me down the aisle, of having him give me away. Do you think it's something he could handle?"

"I think he'd be honored. Give me an invitation and I'll make sure he gets it."

True to her promise, Sam managed to find her father and give him the invitation. For a week Tar wondered how he'd respond. Would he ignore the invitation? Would he be angry she'd attempted to contact him after all this time?

She finally got her answer in the way of a small, but elegant congratulations card. Inside, in scraggly handwriting, she read:

*I am deeply touched by your invitation. I thought you'd forgotten all about me. I would be proud to be at your wedding and honored to give you away.*

*Your loving father.*

# Chapter 20

The church bells chimed Taryn's arrival. Sitting in the backseat of a classic white model-T, Tar clung to her mother's hand. Her father hadn't made it to the apartment as they had agreed and she now wondered if he'd show up at all.

"Why didn't he come? For once in my life I relied on him and..."

"Don't let this upset you, honey. This is your big day."

Tar stepped out of the antique car and looked up at the imposing cathedral. It was spectacular. Never in her wildest dreams would she have thought she'd find herself at the steps of something so monumental; not only the cathedral, but the ceremony to come. The many guests in attendance, including Matt, Henri and several professors, took pictures of her before turning to enter the church.

"Ready?" Sam said.

In her father's absence, Sam had agreed to walk her down the aisle.

As the crowd dissipated and disappeared inside, one man, freshly shaven and wearing a cheap, but clean suit, stood beside Bobby nervously holding a small bouquet of flowers. Though life had clearly been hard on him, the resemblance between father and son was unmistakable.

"Dad?" Taryn said in a disbelieving hush.

"Sorry I didn't meet you at the apartment like we said. I lost the address, but I remembered the church."

"The important thing is that you're here now." She climbed the few steps that brought her face to face with the man who'd been such a horrible father.

He glanced at her beautiful bouquet then down at his simple one. "I guess you won't be needing these."

He was about to toss them aside when Tar reached out to him. "They're beautiful." She handed her bouquet to her mother and took her father's flowers. "They're perfect."

"You sure turned into a smart and beautiful young lady."

"Thanks."

"No thanks to me."

"I guess in your own way you had a hand in who I've become."

He shifted and chuckled uncomfortably. "I'm so sorry for all I did to you. You deserved better."

"I don't want to live in the past. Today's a new day, the start of a whole new life for me, and I'm happy you're here to share it with me." She hooked her arm into his and turned toward the doors of the cathedral. "I think everyone is waiting for us."

Sam and Bobby entered first which cued the bridal march.

Tar steadied her father's trembling hand. "I can't wait for you to meet my husband," she said with a smile.

# Epilogue

The sun was high and hot as Tar and Errol strolled hand in hand through the lush fields of Nana's vineyards. While they could have honeymooned anywhere in the world, Hawaii, New Zealand, Thailand, Greece, they'd both longed for the peace and serenity of the land Errol held so dear. He'd come full circle, finding and losing love until he'd found Tar.

"So when are we going to start bottling our own wine?" Tar said as she reached out for a plump, juicy grape. "I've always wanted my own wine."

"You'd have to find a name for it."

"How 'bout, *Le Petit Fils*," she said with a smile as she popped the grape in her mouth.

"Nana would have loved that... The Grandson... sounds nicer in French."

"It does have a nice ring to it. Leaning into him, she shot him a teasing glance as she rubbed her belly with her free hand. "And maybe it's not only wine that we'll make."

He stopped suddenly and looked at her, his eyes narrow in confusion and restrained joy. "Are you saying...?"

She playfully slapped his arm and laughed, pulling him onward through the vineyard. "Not yet, no, but I'm optimistic. By next year I hope to have a little Tarie or Erroline running around here."

Again he stopped and looked solemnly at her. "Are you sure you're okay with living out here? In France? Are you sure you're ready to leave New York behind... the restaurant, your family?"

"You're my family now, Errol, and I want to go wherever you go, wherever you're happy. Of course I'll miss my family, but we can always fly to New York a few times a year, and it'd be great to have them here every once in a while. Maybe for the holidays. It'll sure be a change of pace from the usual Christmas parties we have back home."

"I already know the feast I will prepare for them. It will be like nothing they've ever seen. And the midnight mass at the town chapel is small, but so moving. I'm sure even Bobby would love it."

"Bobby," Tar said as she threw back her head to laugh. "Can you imagine him here, in France, in Paris? All the beautiful women. He wouldn't know which way to look." At the thought of her little Casanova brother, her eyes misted. Despite the joy she found with Errol, she did miss him and her mother.

Errol reached into his pocket and pulled out his phone.

"What is that for?" she said, confused by his actions.

"Well," he said, affecting the tone of a patient teacher to a slow student. "This is a phone, and when you press the proper numbers here, it rings at the other end and you can talk to whomever you like."

She shot him a silly grin. "I know what it's for. What are you showing it to me for?"

"Ah, the importance of asking the right question at the right time."

Giving him a shove with her hips, she almost sent him toppling over. After he regained his balance, he held the phone up to her again. "Call him. Call your mother. Call them and invite them over."

"But, Errol, this is our honeymoon. Surely you don't want them..."

"We've been on a honeymoon for over a month. It's time you reconnect more with your family. Call them. I'm sure they'd love to see how you're settling into the married life."

She took the phone from him, and it instantly rang in her hand. Startled, she looked at the display and gasped. "It's Bobby," she mouthed as she took the call. "Bobby, hi! We were just talking about you."

"All bad, I hope."

"Of course, little brother. What're you up to?"

"Well, right now I'm strolling in front of L'Institute Culinaire de..."

"Paris?" she excitedly finished for him.

"How d'you guess?"

"Bobby, you're in Paris?"

"With Mom right here by my side. She is cramping my style, but she's fun to have around all the same."

"But...how... what are..?" Again her eyes misted over at the thought of her family so close by. She looked over at Errol, who gave her a knowing smile.

"I've decided to enroll. I start in three weeks."

"Bobby, that's great. You're just a few hours away from us. You have to come by to see us."

"I thought you'd never ask."

After giving him the directions, Tar hung up and looked into Errol's loving gaze.

"Did you have something to do with this?"

Errol shrugged. "What?"

"Why would Bobby and Mom be here on our honeymoon?"

"He shows tremendous promise, Taryn, and it appears there is a need for my class to balance out a bit…too many girls in there. Need some testosterone."

"So Bobby's in your class now?" Taryn asked.

"One and another in pastry, and then…"

"Madame X?" Taryn's mouth flew open. She wondered how Bobby would handle her.

"Perhaps…perhaps not…I heard she decided to go to Switzerland for a semester. We'll see." Errol's eyes twinkled with mischief. "So, are you homesick now?"

Taryn reached up to kiss him. "Everyone I love is here. Why would I be homesick? As I said, dear husband, home is wherever you will be."

"As home is where my heart lies, and where it lies is with you. Always. Forever, my beautiful wife," Errol gazed lovingly into her eyes.

Looking at Errol's handsome face, Taryn couldn't imagine being anywhere else. Everything she'd ever wanted in the world was coming together. Silently, she took Errol by the hand, guided him inside where she showed him once again, before their guests arrived, just how much she loved him.

## The World of the Master Chefs Continues (Where Books are Sold) in:

### Bobby's Story in:

HEAT Vol. 1

HEAT Vol. 2

HEAT Vol. 3

HEAT Vol. 4

HEAT Vol. 5

New York Heat (HEAT Vol. 6)

### Leopold Lee's Story in:

Girl Unassumed

### The Kings Brothers:

Stone King

**Kailin Gow**

Brutal King
Broken King

**A Sneak Peak at:**

# The Innocent

## The Protege #2

Kailin Gow

# Prologue

Serena ran through the school as fast as her four inch heels and pencil skirt permitted. It was impossible to be discreet as her heels clicked loudly on the tiled floor of the deserted hall and she felt certain every student in every class could hear her pass by. Everyone was already in their classes where they belonged; everyone except Serena who was thirty minutes late for her very first class.

She pulled open the door to the grand lecture hall and quietly found a seat at the back of the room. Breathless and eager to catch up on what she'd missed, she pulled out her laptop and took notes.

Her quick and quiet entrance, however, didn't go unnoticed by the devastatingly handsome man speaking to the class. He stopped speaking for the slightest second, a pause barely perceptible, but Serena noticed. She also noticed the longing gaze he briefly directed at her.

"Inspiration comes in many forms," he said. "Tragedy and heartache have inspired countless melancholy melodies, whereas joy and romance have brought about beautiful music; music that lifts the spirit; music that brings on the desire to love."

Serena typed out every word, all while keeping her eyes steadily on him. When his gaze swept across the room and stopped to connect with hers for the briefest moment, she didn't see the masterful composer who spoke so eloquently about his passion for music, but a man who loved and needed love. Even with a room full of students between them, she felt his love.

"Some dare say," he went on, "if you've not lived, if you've not lost, you cannot compose great music. True, a life rich with experience, pain and pleasure, gain and loss, love and hate, can beget profound melodies that evoke strong emotions even from the coldest and disinterested listener. However, this doesn't preclude you, young and virginal, green and pure, to compose beautiful music. Everyone has a past, be it filled with sorrow or joy, pride or regret. Don't be afraid to dig deep, to go behind doors you may have closed, to re-open old wounds you'd rather forget. Pour them out onto that blank sheet of paper staring back at you."

He turned his back on the room and walked to the piano set behind him. Sitting down, he looked at the room of eager students. "If you would humor me, please close your eyes, listen, and allow your emotions to take over."

With one finger, he tapped on a solitary low note for two measures before adding a slow and dramatic melody.

Serena closed her eyes and listened to every note. She could almost hear his voice calling out to her as his fingers played along the lower register of the piano. She could almost hear his heart break.

The melody ached, broke and fell apart with devastating heartache. As the song went on, brooding and dark, she heard a few sniffles, a few whimpers and finally a soft sob.

When Sebastian rested his fingers over the stilled keys of the piano, the room was silent save for the quiet sobs. Serena opened her eyes and caught Sebastian's poignant gaze, a gaze filled with the very emotions his composition evoked. His blue eyes held her, mesmerized as the emotions filled her.

"Now," Sebastian said with a clap of his hands. He cleared his throat and stood before the class. "Looking at you, I can see there's plenty of emotion in the room. What did you feel?"

"Sad," many students said at once.

"Yes," Sebastian said. "I guess there is something rather sad about it. Anything else?"

"The rhythm was almost plaintive, as if the piano was crying."

"Some of the combinations of low base notes with the high, sharp ones added something mysterious and enigmatic to the melody."

"I felt sad, almost morose throughout the song, but in the end, it seemed to hold a faint note of hope."

Sebastian cocked his brow. "Interesting. So we have a sad mystery with a grain of hope."

"Where did you get the inspiration for such a composition?" a young woman in the front row said.

Wringing his hands together, Sebastian shot a wicked grin around the large room. He inhaled deeply as he hesitated. "All I'll say is, when you find love, true love, hold onto it, because once you let go, it can easily become your greatest regret in life."

"Are you in love with someone you can't have?" another girl asked.

He grinned and clucked his tongue. "I'm happy to see my music touched you all as intended. Think about what you can bring to your own compositions and I'll see you all tomorrow."

Having dismissed the question and the class, Sebastian picked up his notes and jacket as students cleared the room. With the room almost empty, he walked to the back of the class to Serena.

"You came in late."

"There was more traffic than I anticipated." She slipped her laptop into her bag and pulled the strap over her shoulder. "I'll make sure I leave home earlier tomorrow."

"You look lovely today – surprisingly prim and proper. I'll admit you're just as alluring buttoned up to the collar as you are in the nude. There's something naughty behind that crisp blue shirt that makes me want to tear it off."

"That wasn't my intention. I wanted to show you I'm serious about my music."

He grinned. "Speaking of which… I need to see you in my office. I want to discuss my expectations. As your advisor, I won't tolerate tardiness, or laziness."

"Yes, Sir." Serena followed him out of the lecture hall.

**Consume Me (The Master Chefs Series #3)**

His strides were long and forceful as he walked out of the building and into the neighboring one where his office was housed. On entering the building, she remembered her first encounter with him. How quickly they'd grown close. How quickly she'd developed such intense affection for him.

Now, as he pushed the door open to let her into his office, she knew she wouldn't have the strength to resist him should he touch her.

"You know how I feel about tardiness." His voice was hard with scorn as he closed the door behind them.

Book 2 of The Protégé, The Innocent is now out!

Book 3 – The Master will be out March 2014.

Another Steamy Adult Novel from Kailin Gow

Bestselling Novel…now available!

# The Protégé

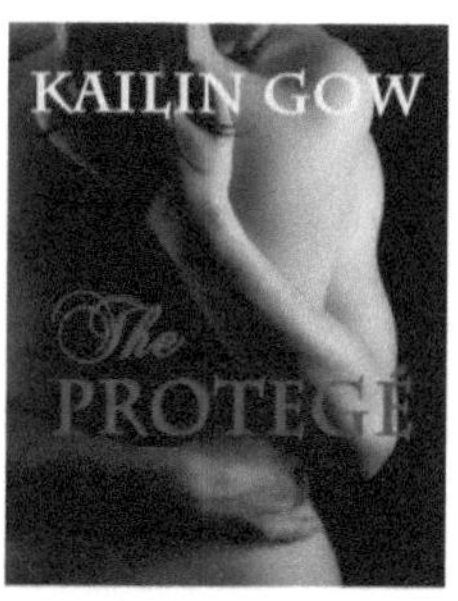


She was the young promising composer in search of a master to teach her and advise her. Serena Singleton was the beautiful up and coming talent brought to the attention of the eccentric, famous, and wildly wealthy Sebastian Sorenson, one of the foremost and most talented composers in Hollywood and in the Academics field. A chance encounter brings them into an arrangement that turns out beyond their expectations and desire, testing their boundaries. Who is the student, the protege, and who is the teacher? Nothing is as it seems in this romantic exotic thriller.

A New Steamy Series from Kailin Gow

For 18+ due to strong sexual situations and mature subject matter

# The Blue Room Trilogy

The Blue Room, an erotic nightclub where the rich and famous go to experience their wildest fantasies, is also the new responsibility of Terrence Blue, the bad boy bastard son of billionaire eccentric Clarence Blue. Terrence, only in his mid-twenties, still has wild oats to sow, drunken parties to attend, and women who bed. Running the exclusive luxury club where discretion is the top priority, then come pleasure, was not what Terrence had planned. He was a client himself, and wanted to stay one, having found his fame and fortune on screen, as one of the biggest stars in the adult films; but finding out that he was son to Clarence Blue, changed all that.

A lot goes on behind the doors of The Blue Room…pleasure, fantasy, betrayal, guilt, and decadence. Everything Terrence is used to, but he never expected that he would find love, too, especially from the least expected...

**A Kailin Gow Adult Novel**

# Get a Free Full-length Book when you subscribe to Kailin's newsletter!

https://dl.bookfunnel.com/5rmis5rrj1

www.ingramcontent.com/pod-product-compliance
Lightning Source LLC
Chambersburg PA
CBHW020411210626
46816CB00006BB/2224
*9781597480826*